WHEN GOD WAS STOLEN

STOLEN

BOOK 2

BY CARY G. OSBORNE

GORDIAN KNOT BOOKS

L ate the third day, [Dzorin] saw a lone tent in the distance. It was a good size, the sort rich merchants and nobles might have. A camel hobbled outside was the only sign of life. The fabric of the tent was richly woven, the camel's trappings expensive. No one hailed him and, certain he wasn't seen, he thought to give the tent a wide berth. However, the silence made him curious about the possibility of a lone traveler of some wealth. There should be a sizable entourage, especially given the tent alone would need one camel to carry it.

He approached the entrance. The late afternoon sun threw his shadow ahead and onto the tent flap.

"Hello," he shouted.

He waited but no one answered. He shouted again. Still no answer. Was it abandoned, or the owners killed by nomads? The camel wouldn't still be there if that was the case. Very slowly, Dzorin raised the flap and, stooping low, went in. The darkness inside blinded his sun-tuned eyes, and the moist heat took his breath away. Waiting for his eyes to adjust, he held his breath and listened. The sounds of heavy breathing confirmed someone was there.

"Hello," Dzorin called not quite so loudly. The interior smelled of stale sweat and vomit.

His eyes adjusted, and he vaguely saw movement at the far end.

"Who's there?" a sleepy voice called.

CHAPTER I

Magan and Dzorin held onto each other in a tight embrace, seemingly unwilling to part. The glow of dawn spread across the sky, the sun bathing them in first light. Behind them, the gates of Sharvik stood open. Everyone was gone, no one to protect, life replaced by silence.

She knew he must leave. Their people, having fled to Hattushah, the capital, needed to know they could come home. This time, Dzorin was leaving home, leaving Magan, so he could tell them. After a year of fighting together to get back, how could they not travel together this time? Watching him go was the hardest thing she had ever done.

However, Magan was adamant. She must stay, waiting for something told to her in a dream. In the dream, Iah, the god of Sharvik, told her someone would come if she was patient. Without Dzorin, though, how could she survive? Loneliness already bore down on her, the sense of loss overwhelming.

She reached up and brushed her fingertips across his cheek, wet with tears. "The time will pass," she said. "More quickly than—"

"Of course," he said, cutting her off. "No more excuses, no more trying to convince me this is necessary."

She lowered her hand. Did he think she was being selfish? In her need to wait alone, to find the teacher, to learn more how to use her abilities and skills, was she being selfish? His duty, on the other hand, was to find their people, bring them home where they belonged. He was the unselfish one, devoted to their people and duty.

Most people would say his decision was more noble, more

unselfish. Yet she had already suffered much for the good of their people. A whole year of their lives spent in trying to find and retrieve Iah, the golden idol, the people's god, in whom she did not believe. Because she wasn't a believer, their fellow villagers, her people, always avoided her. Even so, she did not hesitate to go out into the desert with a fellow warrior, into the unknown, where they both suffered and nearly died more than once.

Magan watched Dzorin walk away without looking back. Tears streamed down her cheeks. Was she losing him forever? Did he understand?

Her hand came up and she opened her mouth to call him back. *Don't go. Don't leave me.*

Instead, she waved goodbye, even though he didn't see. He disappeared over the first small hill into the desert and she remained. Was it worth this separation, even if a teacher did come?

She stepped inside and closed the gates but didn't bar them. There was no need for the protection they provided with everyone gone, and they would only keep out the teacher. She returned to her home to prepare for whatever was to happen. Not knowing how or when someone would appear, she decided to meditate, look inward at her goals and needs. Try to calm her spirit, now in such turmoil. Dark and cavernous, the temple was the best place, empty now of religious paraphernalia, worshipers, and priests.

As she gathered together what she needed to take with her, she considered events leading to this moment. The raiders coming in the night to steal the idol from the temple. The search for Iah, the god of the village. The dangers, both physical and mental. The sounds of battle, echoing from the walls, through the lanes and alleys.

In the encounters with Friya, high priestess in Mari, she discovered her own magic was strong, as were her skills in the martial arts, yet there were too many stumbles and hesitations. She faltered, not knowing what to do next, or exactly what she was capable of. She and Dzorin managed to make it back to their homes only to find the people gone. Settling back in was impossible, of course. Their fellows must return, and it was up to the two of them to make it happen.

Instead, she was staying behind, because Iah came to her in a dream while she slept in Dzorin's arms several nights before. She'd told Dzorin about the dream, about the promise it made. Was it hubris to believe someone would come just because she needed them? That by reaching out with her mind, she would be heard?

What if no one heard?

Dzorin's mind still full of memories and hardships they had shared, emotions churning inside him, continued walking. He had known Magan all of his life, yet she often surprised him during those months they traveled together. They grew close after leaving Sharvik more than a year ago, hoping to find and recover the golden idol stolen from the temple that horrible night.

Memories came to him often, the shouting and panic, and the shame all of the warriors felt when they learned Iah, their god, was taken. They had fought bravely but were heavily outnumbered. Magan, the only woman warrior among them, fought as heroically as the men. She who defied the priests and the god, left with Dzorin the next day, to find and bring god back to their people.

And they found it. The golden idol was taken from the mercenaries, and now lay buried in the sand of a riverbed, still well hidden they hoped, until the two of them could lead their people to uncover him and bring him home.

But their return was not easy. Captured by slave merchants, sold separately, they ended up in Mari where they were forced to participate in a reenactment of a battle between the gods before the whole city where Magan had been placed in the high priestess's household.

They escaped from the city, pursued by the high priestess, Friya of Mari, a witch who could change her appearance at will. Using her own magical powers, Magan overcame the witch time and again. In the end, Friya seduced Dzorin in the guise of Kira, a beautiful young woman held captive by a tribe of nomads and condemned to death.

The devotion between him and Magan nearly broke apart. In the end, their feelings for each other grew until they knew they loved one another. After the months of hardship, they made it back to Sharvik, only to find the village deserted.

He stopped abruptly and looked back. In such a confused state, he was much farther from the gates than he realized. Both they and Magan were out of sight. When would he see their home again? More importantly, when would he see Magan again?

CHAPTER 2

Magan carried what she needed to the temple, the place where she once fought dead warriors when the priests had denounced her. After placing two lit oil lamps on the dais where Iah once sat, she spread a blanket on the floor in the same place as on the night when the dead warriors appeared. It seemed so long ago.

Amleth, high priest, had challenged her to spend one night in the temple by herself. She agreed, naming conditions she thought would prevent the priests from cheating. Through some sort of magic, she was set upon by the dead warriors of Sharvik, rising from a mist spreading across the floor.

Wearing armor over their skeletal remains and weapons in their bony hands, they attacked. One by one she fought them. She couldn't kill them; they were already dead. But for the rest of the night, she managed to hold them off.

She shook off the memory of the sound of blade striking blade, the echoes bouncing from the walls of the chamber and arranged the things she brought with her. On one side of the blanket lay her bronze sword, battered from many fights. On the other side, a jug of water and her cape.

Looking around at the darkness of the chamber, she let her eyes adjust. Amleth died the night the mercenaries attacked. Niches, corners, and shelves sat empty. If the god was real, wouldn't he still be there, in spite of the idol being leagues away? And the priests—was their belief so fragile they gave up once the idol was gone? She didn't believe in the gods and saw priests as parasites, feeding off the needs of the people, but the beliefs of the representatives of Iah should be stronger. They all gave up, the priests and the people, while she, an unbeliever faced death to find him. Would they see her differently now?

She shook off the doubts and took a long drink of water. The flames of the small lamps flickered in the draft, mere points of reference in the vast darkness. Why were temples so often without openings for light to enter?

Walls, columns, and altar blended into the darkness as if they never existed. Memories of ghosts were all that remained.

She often dreamed of walking into the temple, vivid, compelling dreams. Everything was in place as if the people never left: the tapestries and sconces for torches, the ewers and bowls on the altar, and golden Iah perched benignly on his pedestal. Looking up, he had smiled and raised his hand to bless her. She blinked, and he was as still as ever. Did she imagine he moved? It was a dream, after all.

Now, the echo of her footsteps was gone, her breathing echoed around the chamber like a whisper. None of the priests hid in the inner sanctum or rooms behind the altar. None of the villagers stood in the sanctuary, praying or waiting for a blessing. Her senses stretched outside, into the homes and the market filled with silence.

In all of the emptiness, she sat expectantly, listening for a footfall, waiting for the air to stir with the presence of another person. Something momentous was about to happen. It was here, in the temple, the next turn in her life would begin.

In spite of the anticipation, her thoughts turned to Dzorin. They had made love the night before, sweetly, passionately, knowing it might be months before they would see each other again. Neither slept much afterward, he because he didn't understand her decision, she because decision would mean in later times.

She had awakened early. The sky showed palely through the open door. Dzorin snored beside her, and grief at their imminent parting had brought tears to her eyes.

Tears came to her eyes again as she prepared to wait in the darkness. A draft sent the flames of the lamps flickering more brightly, setting shadows dancing on the walls and columns. The draft caught the smoke and carried it away from her. Sitting cross-legged on the blanket, she took a deep breath, and cleared her mind.

She stood up once during the day, working out a cramp in her calf and getting a drink from the waterskin. In the afternoon, her mind turned fully inward. For the rest of the day and the night, she sat, not knowing what to expect, hoping for the best, fearing the worst.

Sharvik's history unfolded rapidly, from before Amleth's anointing as high priest to the night Iah was stolen. The vision expanded to include Hattushah, the capital, where the gods demanded even the king give them homage.

Warfare and death devastated the land, but it revived, shaking off the effects of human foolishness. People and places appeared, far from her desert, strange and meaningless. Spectacles of pomp and encounters, both violent and peaceful. People were maimed and killed or raised to political or military heights.

Voices screamed in the night and Iah moved away from Sharvik in a wooden cart. The raiders disappeared. People wept after him.

In the moonlight, a glint of gold sparkled from the sand. Iah was slightly uncovered, a small part of him revealed to the world.

Magan snapped awake. Her eyes focused slowly. Sitting on the floor before her was a woman dressed in a green wool robe and leather sandals. A fur was wrapped around her shoulders. Her hair was grey and long, hanging straight down her back, except for a thick braid hanging over one shoulder. Her face was serene, eyes closed, as if she slept. Her hands rested in her lap, long fingers entwined. The most remarkable thing of all was her pale skin, very like the white warriors who served Friya.

The woman's eyes opened slowly. Even in the gloom of the temple, their blue, like the sky overhead, shone. It was an eye color Magan had never seen before. "You waken at last," the woman said in a voice so soft it was difficult to hear.

Magan shivered, feeling energy flow from this woman as powerfully as she once felt from Friya. She was instantly suspicious.

"Why have you summoned me?" the woman said.

"I summoned you?" she said. "I don't even know you." Her question rang hollow even in her own ears. What had she been doing with all of the meditation if not calling out to a teacher?

"You are a novice," the woman said. Her eyebrows arched. "I have never felt such a strong call from someone totally unschooled."

"Who are you?" Magan asked.

"My name is Brynja. I am a teacher."

Silently, they studied each other. In her dreams, Iah told her to wait. A teacher would come although there were moments when she doubted her own feelings. So, this Brynja was the one she sought?

"And you are?" Brynja asked.

"My name is Magan."

"This is your home?"

"Yes. Well, the village is called Sharvik and I live here."

"No one else does?"

"They did. The people left several months ago." Magan was beginning to resent the questions, although it was perfectly logical for the blue-eyed woman to want to know where they were and why. "It's a long story."

"There's time." Brynja stood and held out a hand to help Magan to her feet. "Let's walk while you tell me."

The woman's grip was firm, and a thrill of energy passed from her to Magan. Instead of alarming, the touch was calming. Magan stooped and gathered her things and led the way out of the temple to her own home where she left the things and invited her guest to leave whatever she chose. Brynja shed the fur wrap and the sword slung on its strap over her shoulder.

Back outside, they wandered the streets while Magan told of the night raid and the taking of the idol. Briefly, she described her and Dzorin's search for Iah, how they found it and buried it in a dry riverbed. She glossed over the adventures while they struggled to return to Sharvik, only to find the people gone.

"It must have been devastating," Brynja said.

Magan nodded. "We went through so much to get home. Finding the village deserted ..."

Brynja stopped and looked around. They were back at the temple. The steps leading to the entrance were covered with dirt and sand. The stones of the street were covered, too. Magan watched her expression as she turned to take in the whole of it. A breeze wafted along the street, the sound punctuating the silence.

"I'm hungry," Brynja said. "Let's get me settled in somewhere, then back to your residence and eat."

Magan suggested they could both bed down in her home. There were two rooms, although only one would normally be a sleep room. Brynja agreed. When they sat down to eat, she added dried fish to the meal of boiled lentils. She asked more questions as they ate. They were subtle, as if part of a conversation between friends who had not seen each other in a long time, and it took a while for Magan to realize she was describing her own experience with both weapons and magic.

Time passed, it grew dark outside. Magan grew more comfortable with both the questions and the way in which they were asked. Eventually she rolled up in her blanket on the floor and went to sleep.

She woke to the sound of a bird singing outside. The sun was above the rooftops to the east when she stepped out. She stretched and yawned, feeling more rested than she had in several days.

The sound of footsteps made her turn. Coming down the alley leading to her home, Brynja carried an armful of weapons. Magan stood stock still, amazed not only at the number of weapons, but also at the strength the woman must have to carry so many.

She rushed forward. "Let me help."

"Thanks."

Together, they carried everything into the sleep room, where a stack of weapons already lay on the floor.

Carefully, Magan laid her load down. "How did you—"

"There are ways."

Magan leaned down and touched pieces she'd never seen before. "What are they?"

"We will get to them. Right now, let's go for a run."

Brynja led the way back outside and took off running at a slow pace. Magan followed, guessing this was her first lesson.

CHAPTER 3

The air was silent and hot. *Put one foot in front of the other,* Dzorin thought. *Don't look back. Don't think.* His mind roiled with conflicting feelings about Magan and his people. He questioned when what he did would be enough. Thoughts and speculations appeared and disappeared, jumping around in his mind. He could stand these doubts and questions no longer. He stopped and looked up. The sun was well past zenith.

This was a route he had never trod before, but everyone in Sharvik knew in what direction the capital lay. Would there be any signs of the villagers' journey so many months earlier?

He shrugged and resumed the journey. What else could he do? Neither the sky nor the earth held any answers. The distance between him and Magan increased with every step. He ignored the urge to turn back.

She had not told him if she was going off on her own or staying within the walls of Sharvik. Wild possibilities plagued him. Not least was the fear she might be punishing him at last for betraying her with Kira, young and beautiful, the alter ego of Friya. He remembered Kira but not the lust or need to protect her.

Would such foolishness never stop haunting him? Even if Magan truly and completely forgave he could neither forgive himself nor forget. In small ways, the memory flavored his every reaction to Magan and his feelings for her. He could wish it never happened, but it was useless, especially with the very frightening possibility Friya did not, could not die.

Friya, a witch, a priestess, a woman bent on revenge against him and Magan. Magan, most particularly. A woman like her could not accept rejection, and Magan rejected her on so many levels. He worried hatred and desire for revenge alone might make her strong enough to survive.

Their encounter with Friya had made Magan doubt her own abilities. Why couldn't she discard all magic as he had? But then he didn't either, did he? He used what he learned as a novice priest against the specters in the haunted village after they escaped Mari. Tricks only, not real power like Magan possessed. Just priestly tricks meant to fool the innocent and hopeful. Amazingly, Friya was fooled.

Dzorin shook himself out of his reverie to see the sun hovering just above the horizon. One nice thing about a mind in turmoil: the body continues with the simple tasks, numbed by fatigue, until the whole person is jolted back to reality. He stopped to eat, mostly dried lentils they found stored in jars and a few onions growing wild in the communal garden in spite of the neglect. In two or three more days, if he remembered correctly, and if nothing untoward happened in recent months, he should come upon a village where he could get a little more food and water. If only he could be sure Magan would have the same good fortune.

The village lay in a shallow basin as he'd expected. It was mid-afternoon of the seventh day and he decided to stay the night if there was no objection. The villagers were friendly and as generous as they could afford to be, giving him bread and fruit and a place to lay his head for the night. They saw few travelers and asked many questions about where he came from and where he was going.

He asked if a large number of people had moved past several months before. They remembered the people of Sharvik, although only the leaders entered their village to ask if camping outside their walls was permissible. Two young men drew water from the well for the animals and to top off their supplies. Dzorin had the impression these people were wary of such a large group passing.

"They stayed two nights," the village headman said. "They topped off their water again and left early morning.

"They did seem very sad," the headman added. "We gathered they'd suffered some sort of great loss."

They didn't say how long they'd traveled, but for such a large caravan to get from Sharvik to this village may have been ten days or more. One of Sharvik's priests had expressed gratitude for their kindness and the water. Dzorin suspected it was Julin who was the most gracious of his group.

His belly full, Dzorin spent the night under the roof of the stable. The second morning, he rose before sunrise. The headman appeared to see him off while he filled his waterskin. Dzorin thanked him for his hospitality and as the sun rose, he started off again. Dzorin resigned himself once more to the lonely trek.

Late the third day, he saw a lone tent in the distance. It was a good size, the sort rich merchants and nobles might have. A camel hobbled outside was the only sign of life. The fabric of the tent was richly woven, the camel's trappings expensive. No one hailed him and, certain he wasn't seen, he thought to give the tent a wide berth. However, the silence made him curious about the possibility of a lone traveler of some wealth. There should be a sizable entourage, especially given the tent alone would need one camel to carry it.

He approached the entrance. The late afternoon sun threw his shadow ahead and onto the tent flap.

"Hello," he shouted.

He waited but no one answered. He shouted again. Still no answer. Was it abandoned, or the owners killed by nomads? The camel wouldn't still be there if that was the case. Very slowly, Dzorin raised the flap and, stooping low, went in. The darkness inside blinded his sun-tuned eyes, and the moist heat took his breath away. Waiting for his eyes to adjust, he held his breath and listened. The sounds of heavy breathing confirmed someone was there.

"Hello," Dzorin said not quite so loudly. The interior smelled of stale sweat and vomit.

His eyes adjusted, and he vaguely saw movement at the far end.

"Who's there?" a sleepy voice called.

"A traveler."

"Wait a moment."

The rasp of striking flint crossed the distance, and a lamp glowed into existence, revealing an old man lying upon and under expensive rugs. His hand shook as it held up the lamp, his face as pale as his unkempt beard and long hair. He stared at Dzorin with watery eyes.

"Thank the gods you have come."

CHAPTER 4

Dzorin sat with a piece of cloth tied around the lower half of his face. The tent was finely made of goat hair and withstood the forces howling outside its walls; the blowing wind made the walls of the tent blow out, then collapse inward with a whoosh. Fine dust filtered through seams and the strands of hair, creating the transparency of a foggy evening in the glow of the two oil lamps burning to one side. If it were raining, the hairs would swell, making the tent watertight.

The smell of stale sweat penetrated the mask. The old man slept fitfully, moaning unintelligible words now and then. His fever still raged after two days. The dark storm made him restless, and twice Dzorin held the man on his bed of rugs and pillows as he flailed around. Afterward, he checked the splint tied from mid-thigh to ankle and the paste holding the skin together where it was slit by the shin bone.

Dzorin dipped a rag in a basin of water, squeezed out the excess, and reapplied the compress to the man's forehead. His patient relaxed, lying perfectly still, showing no further reaction to his savior's ministrations.

When Dzorin first stepped into the tent, the man was lucid enough to say his leg was broken. The camel had fallen, landing on top of him. Thinking he would die, the men he hired for the journey moved him into the tent already set up. They'd taken the other camels and the best items he'd carried. Why they left the camel that fell on him, the merchant didn't know. It wasn't hurt in the fall.

A search of the tent turned up a supply of water, food, cloth to tear into strips for bandages and compresses, and a few herbs. Dzorin talked as he gathered everything.

"My name is Dzorin. I come from a village called Sharvik."

"I am Lahnlee of Acre," came the response through gritted teeth.

Dzorin had never heard of Acre and asked where it lay. It was a city-state on the coast to the south. Lahnlee described the city as Dzorin worked.

"I will have to set the leg," Dzorin said when all was ready. "Is there any wine?"

"Over there." Lahnlee motioned weakly.

Dzorin found several jugs piled with other items the men had left behind. He found one with the wax seal broken and removed the clay stopper. The fragrance was of a strong wine, which was good. A search through belongings piled in the same corner, uncovered a cup. He poured out a generous amount.

He supported the old man with an arm around his shoulders. Lahnlee nearly choked drinking it all down. A second cup went down more easily. Dzorin took a long drink himself, dreading what he must do.

While the wine worked its own sort of magic, Dzorin went to the camel pack lying beside the entrance and took it apart. It yielded three short poles for a splint and a long leather strap he cut into four strips. He ripped expensive garments into lengths for bandages and carried everything to the bed of carpets.

He was taught how to set broken bones as an acolyte in the priesthood as part of the supposed training in magic. The people knew nothing of such things, and when the priests were able to cure an illness or mend a broken leg, they were impressed. To promote the awe people felt, priests never revealed how healing was done. Although he decided not to be a priest, choosing to join the scouts instead, he retained much of what he learned.

Dzorin had handed Lahnlee one of the leather straps. "Bite on this when I tell you."

The old man nodded and took the strap.

Dzorin sat on a pillow to raise himself to the same level as the merchant, placed the poles and cloth strips within easy reach, and studied the jagged edge of the shinbone shining through the torn skin. This break wasn't going to just snap back into place. What was the best way to approach it?

The smell of sweat and fear had assailed his nostrils more strongly. It must be his own. However, if he was going to do it, he'd better start. He placed a thick wad of cloth against Lahnlee's groin and took off his own sandals. He placed the injured leg between both of his own with his bare foot braced against the man's groin. He grasped the swollen ankle with both hands.

"Now," he said, waited a moment, and pulled, slowly increasing the pressure.

Lahnlee groaned past the strap between his teeth. Sweat broke out all over Dzorin's body and ran into his eyes. His hands slipped slightly, and he tightened his grip. The exposed bone sank inward. If only his hands didn't slip further.

A grinding sound came from the leg. Lahnlee had screamed and passed out. Chills raised the hair on the back of Dzorin's neck. The wound began bleeding again, but the bone disappeared under the skin. Dzorin kept up the pressure a little longer to ensure the two ends did not separate before he got the splint bound in place.

His left hand slipped suddenly off the ankle down to the heel. He fell over on his right elbow, rolled onto his back until his breathing slowed. He rested another moment. The job wasn't over.

He got up, wiped blood away from the wound, and inspected the shin. It looked good. With luck it should heal, although the leg might never be as strong as before. He had mixed yarrow powder from a chest of herbs and spices with honey and spread it over the open wound to keep it from becoming infected. Further treatment would have to wait until they reached civilization and found a more experienced physician.

He placed the poles around the leg and tied them in place with cloth strips from ankle to mid-thigh. Now, they could settle down to wait.

In the meantime, he scrounged through the piles of things and found everything he needed to survive the next few days. Large jugs of water, dried fruit among other foodstuffs, and more wine. Oil for the lamps was stored in small clay jugs. At least those who left the wounded man on his own didn't take everything.

He couldn't help wondering why the men left so much behind. Did they want to be able to say they left enough for his survival and it wasn't their fault if he died? Perhaps they worked for him before and liked the merchant. It didn't make sense. Perhaps Lahnlee could say when he was lucid.

For two days, the wounded man raved feverishly. Each day, Dzorin reapplied the paste to the wound. The second day, the dust storm came, increasing the injured man's discomfort. He raved until the fever broke, almost at the same time the storm ceased. He lay exhausted, drank large amounts of water, and began eating the day after. Dzorin chafed at the delay, eager to get to Hattushah and find his people, but he couldn't just leave the man as the hired men had. The older man's condition would have to improve before they could move on. At least the tent proved to be a good shelter during the storm.

Dzorin came to know the merchant during the two days the storm lasted and the next three days. Lahnlee was fifty-eight years old and a merchant of some wealth. As a young man, he had traveled the known world, seen and done many things.

As they waited for Lahnlee to get strong enough to travel in short stages, he told Dzorin stories from his life. Over the years, he visited every major city in the Tigris and Euphrates lands and sailed along the seacoast to Egypt and Anatolia. He described different objects he had carried on this trip, things now gone, telling where each came from. Some were for his own use; most were merchandise he was transporting to Hattushah to sell.

It came as no surprise he was headed for Hattushah since it was the next large city along this route. They discussed why the men he'd hired made sure to leave everything he needed but took off with the rest of the goods and the other camels. The animal left behind suffered no injury in the fall, but he suspected the crew didn't realize or they would have taken it, too.

"They were all good men," he said of his crew. "I hired many of them over the years, but I couldn't expect them to stay with me, not knowing how long it might take for me to either heal or die."

Dzorin didn't believe a rich merchant would be so forgiving of their deserting him in his greatest time of need. He didn't question aloud, though, since it was none of his business.

As the healing continued, plans needed to be made for continuing on to Hattushah. A single camel could not carry everything the thieves left behind plus a full-grown man, no matter how much weight he lost. Once the storm spent its power and the tent could be opened to daylight, Dzorin spent a day sorting through Lahnlee's possessions, selecting those things to carry with them and those to leave behind.

Occasionally, he became distracted by the beauty or uniqueness of the merchandise. Twice he asked Lahnlee what things were or what they were used for. In a crate of particularly beautiful items, he came upon a dagger of unusual workmanship. He held it up to the light coming through the tent opening, watching sunlight play over the gold and small inlaid jewels of the scabbard.

"You may have it if you wish," Lahnlee said.

"Oh, no. It's much too valuable."

"A thank you for saving my life."

"I ..." He looked at it. He pulled the blade free and tested its edge. It was sharper than anything he had seen in the armory in Sharvik. The handle was of some animal horn with a large blue opaque stone set in the hilt. It was a fine weapon, both beautiful and useful.

"Please, accept it," Lahnlee said.

Dzorin looked from the merchant and back to the weapon. It was such a generous gift, one he couldn't turn down. With a nod and a "thank you," he slipped it under his belt under the long tunic.

For the nights to come, Dzorin put together a smaller, makeshift tent using some of the rugs. Once the large tent was struck, the tentpoles would be cut the right length for the smaller version. When the small tent was taken apart, it became a litter Lahnlee could lie on, pulled behind the camel.

The night before they left, he dug out a large space in the sand. Next morning, he laid the flattened tent in the depression and placed the items on it they were leaving behind, tied the corners together, and anchored the whole thing with some of the tent pegs. He weighed down the edges with stones he'd gathered earlier and shoveled sand over the whole thing until it could not be seen, adding more in hopes the wind wouldn't uncover the cache. Lahnlee might return for it someday. Even if he didn't, or it was gone when he did, the items would be protected for a time. The desert would not treat the items kindly in the meantime, but he hoped for the best.

The merchant was short and had been stocky before his injury. On the litter behind the camel, he now looked thin, wizened, and unsteady. With his weakened condition, they started early in the morning when it was cooler. They traveled slowly, stopping to rest and eat at noon. Two hours later, they moved on, continuing for at least another two hours. Lahnlee endured the discomfort silently for the most part, cursing occasionally when the jostling caused grater pain. Over the days, he proved to be a pleasant companion in spite of the pain and inconvenience of his broken leg.

At the end of the fourth day of travel, the evening meal over and each with a cup of wine in hand, they sat talking. A breeze blew softly, cooling and fresh. They fell silent, listening to the light rattle of the skittering sand.

"I left home in search of my youngest son," Lahnlee said after a time. "He disappeared somewhere in this part of the world. I thought perhaps someone in the capital could help me find him. Tarn was a soldier and he got involved in some mercenary army."

Involved how? Dzorin wondered. Mercenaries usually meant raiders.

"How long ago did he disappear?" he asked, aloud.

"Over a year now. His friends and the captain were not too clear on exactly when or where."

"Could he have been killed?"

"No one knows. That's the strange thing. He simply disappeared one night after the merchant caravan he was guarding set up camp. Everyone was asleep, all was quiet, like now. An idol they carried also disappeared without a trace. It was not very big, but sheathed in gold as it was, the thing was very heavy." Lahnlee shook his head sadly. "The superstitious fools thought the god escaped and took Tarn in revenge. Maybe they're right. I've been searching for three months and haven't found a single clue."

"I would have thought they could tell you where this happened," Dzorin said.

Lahnlee shrugged. "You would think so."

Dzorin stood abruptly. "I'd better see to the camel. And you'd better get some rest."

He helped the older man crawl into the tent, just big enough for him to stretch out full-length. Once he was settled, Dzorin strode into the night, his thoughts in a tangle. Instead of going directly to the camel, he rounded the tent and climbed the hillock behind it, where he sat down, sifting sand between his fingers.

By all the gods, how had such an encounter happened? Tarn must be the soldier buried with Iah. Anything else would be too much of a coincidence. More so than meeting the father of the man he'd helped to murder a year ago?

Was it really possible? Had he saved the life of the father of the dead mercenary?

Those moments haunted him, came to him in his dreams, and sometimes when he least expected it, he would see the hulking warrior in his mind's eye. He never saw his face, couldn't remember if he'd seen it clearly in the darkness of the night and the rush of fear.

He often remembered the horror of burying the dead man in the same hole in which they hid Iah as much as the horror of killing him. The idol was much too heavy to move without a wagon or cart. It was Magan's idea to bury the golden idol and return to Sharvik to gather enough people to return him to the village. Vanthi, a fellow warrior sent out from the village in a different direction to track down their god, was still alive then. They had met a day before finding the raiders. Getting the idol off the wagon and dragging it under the tent to the dry riverbed took all the strength the three of them possessed, although he knew now Magan helped with her powers. After they buried the idol and the mercenary who he now suspected was named Tarn, everything went bad. After more than a year, he was still trying to bring the stolen god home to his people.

Should he tell Lahnlee how his son had died and where he was buried? If he didn't, the old man would never know. The journey to Hattushah would last another two or three days at their current rate of travel. There was enough time to decide what to do.

He threw down a handful of sand, circled back, and fed the camel. Rolled up in a rug and his cloak, he slept very little.

CHAPTER 5

The crowds appeared on the road late morning. Within a few leagues, hundreds of people came and went. Dzorin and Lahnlee made their own way slowly toward the city's open gates, other travelers passing them, some cursing their slow pace. None of them traveled as far as the two dusty, tired men, no more tired than the camel carrying Lahnlee and his belongings. Dzorin gripped the animal's lead to prevent the press of people from separating them.

They had made better time the past two days, as the old man grew stronger, in spite of the rigors of traveling. The trip was a hard one, each day and night filled with Lahnlee's pain, although he tried to hide it. The pain eased gradually, he still did not sleep well.

Dzorin's own pain from the knowledge Tarn was Lahnlee's son, plagued his thoughts with each step. He worried over whether to tell the merchant and, if so, how or when to do it. Arriving in Hattushah meant there was little more time to decide.

Lahnlee knew where to find lodgings within the walls.

"I visited this city with my caravans when I was younger. Not so much in the past few years, my route taking me farther south. But cities like this don't change very much in so short time."

Dzorin agreed to help him as far as a place to stay. Once Lahnlee was settled in, Dzorin would set out in search of his own people. Over the many days trekking across the desert, he told the old man of his quest for his people with as few details as possible. It occurred to him, once he knew Lahnlee and the dead warrior were related, the last thing he wanted was for the merchant to know where Sharvik was located, should he decide to seek revenge.

Lahnlee had spoken often in the evenings of finding his son as they ate and prepared for sleep. The mere mention of Tarn's name now set Dzorin's teeth on edge, tightened his jaws. There was no doubt the guard buried with Iah was Tarn. Nor did he doubt Lahnlee would seek revenge for his death.

After they passed through the gates and into the city, their pace was slowed further by the narrow alleys and the sheer numbers of people, animals, and carts. The odors assailing their nostrils would be familiar to anyone entering any city: food, spices, animal droppings, unwashed bodies, perfumes. The only city Dzorin knew to compare this to was Mari, which to his mind was more sophisticated.

"Turn left here," Lahnlee called down, pointing toward a narrower lane off to the left.

Dzorin led the camel across the stone surface of the road. The size of the animal forced the smaller donkeys and people to stop and let them pass, amid a few curses and ancient gestures. Once in the narrow side street, they moved quickly along its near emptiness. Noise from the main avenue diminished behind them, never disappearing entirely, while Lahnlee directed Dzorin through more narrow streets and alleys, leading into the city's interior.

"You have been this way before," Dzorin said.

Lahnlee peered ahead intently, memory guiding him. "Many times, but memory can be tricky. Right up here, I think," he said a few minutes later. "Yes. Stop here."

The entrance directly in front of Dzorin bore a sign indicating it was a tavern named the Crowing Rooster. As far from the gates as it was, a traveler would have to know of its existence in advance.

"Help me up."

Dzorin made the camel crouch down and held Lahnlee's hands, easing him to his feet in a maneuver they had become adept at. Leaning on the younger man's arm on one side and a walking stick on the other, Lahnlee led the way inside. It took a minute for their eyes to adjust to the darker interior. Three men seated at a table in the corner looked up for a moment, then returned to the game they were playing with pieces so worn they were featureless. The newcomers chose a table near the door and sat waiting. Soon, a serving girl appeared from a room in the back.

"Wine?"

"Yes, please," answered Lahnlee. "And I would like to see the landlord."

She nodded, went first to a shelf to the side, and poured wine into two wooden cups. She set the cups on the table and waited. Lahnlee pulled a copper coin from his belt and placed it in her hand. Without another word, she disappeared into a back room. Another minute and a very large man appeared through the same doorway and approached their table.

"One of you wants to see me?" His voice was as deep as his body was broad.

"Yes," Lahnlee replied. "I'm looking for lodgings for a few days while I conduct some business here. You have rooms?"

"Upstairs."

"How much?"

"Three coppers a day."

Lahnlee nodded. "Reasonable enough. Including meals, of course."

The landlord looked argumentative for an instant then nodded.

"Would you help my friend bring in my things? Oh, and the camel needs to be stabled."

"For a copper."

Lahnlee smiled faintly. "Done."

He handed over the coins, and Dzorin led the way outside. He unloaded the bags and pulled the wooden frame free. The landlord picked up most of it at one time and carried the belongings into the building and up the stairs. Following behind, Dzorin deposited his lesser load on the floor of the airless room. Once the window was opened and air was allowed to circulate, it would be more comfortable. He rejoined his companion.

They sat in silence for several minutes, finishing their wine. It occurred to Dzorin he could remain with the merchant and help him his first few days in the city. However, the knowledge he must impart to the older man weighed heavily on him and he wanted to get the telling of it over. Once the tale was told, there was no reason for Dzorin to remain. The merchant still possessed enough coins to sustain him for months, and Dzorin wondered again how he'd managed to prevent his former crew from stealing it all.

The wench, possibly the landlord's daughter, could be depended on to run a few errands for Lahnlee or to get some boy off the street to do it, and he would probably have no trouble hiring a man or two for whatever else needed doing. Dzorin was eager to begin his search for the villagers, but without coins for lodging or food, staying was a strong temptation. However, his plan had always been to go about his own business once they reached Hattushah.

He felt a strong bond between them and dreaded destroying it. The old man was dying when he found him. He survived because of Dzorin's care, and he felt responsible for Lahnlee's safety. But it was senseless to prolong the moment.

"I appreciate all you have done," Lahnlee broke into his thoughts. "I could not have made it without you. You must be eager to begin your search."

Dzorin looked at him squarely. He wasn't exactly being dismissed. He could stay for a while.

"You have been a good companion," he said, then hesitated, not wanting to destroy the relationship with the words he felt he must say. "There is something I must tell you."

Lahnlee's eyebrows rose slightly, and he studied Dzorin's face. He drank the last of his wine and waited.

"Your son," he said. "I know where Tarn is buried."

Lahnlee looked startled, and it was a moment before he spoke.

"How?" His tone was suspicious, his voice low and harsh.

"Because I helped to bury him."

Lahnlee's eyes widened. His voice shook when he spoke. "Did you also help to kill him?"

"Yes." Dzorin kept his gaze steady. When the old man said nothing more, he continued. "I told you of the raid on the village when Iah was stolen. It took weeks to catch up with the raiders. When we sneaked the idol off the wagon and out of the tent, a guard caught us. It must have been Tarn. He was poised to kill us. My companions and I …"

Lahnlee's gaze was intense. His jaw muscles worked as he gritted his teeth. He must be torn between anger at this revelation and gratitude for saving his life.

"You're just now realizing it was Tarn?"

"No. It was clear days ago."

"And you continued to act …"

Dzorin sighed. There was nothing he could have done then, and there was nothing he could do now to change what happened.

Lahnlee sat silently, his eyes cast down, his jaw muscles still visibly working as he digested the story. His fingers turned a copper over and over.

"I will come back here in a few days and give you whatever details you want. I can show you where he is buried or bring his body to you. I have to return to the area anyway."

Angry silence became a wall between the two men.

Dzorin sighed with regret. "I am sorry about your son, Lahnlee. At the time, there was no choice." He stood and started out.

"Dzorin!"

He turned just as Lahnlee tossed the copper in his direction. He caught it, holding both it and his temper tightly.

"For your services," Lahnlee said without expression.

Dzorin nodded and walked out of the building. To Lahnlee, the giving and accepting of the coin ended any friendship between them. Behind Dzorin now sat an implacable enemy who, in spite of the hardships shared for the past several days, would not forgive the death of his son.

He patted the camel as he turned into the lane, wondering if he would keep his promise to return, then disappeared into the maze of streets and alleys. As he adjusted his tunic and cloak, his hand brushed against the knife in his belt, the gift from Lahnlee for saving his life. He should return it and for a moment he thought of going back.

He changed his mind, reasoning it would be better to leave Lahnlee alone for now. He could return the knife when he came back to the inn.

CHAPTER 6

No one in the city seemed to know of villagers from the east who came to the capital several months ago. Dzorin tried to see the city prefect and to get into a meeting of the council of elders, but the prefect was away for several days and the meeting was a closed one and he was turned away.

After a second night of sitting in an alley with his back against a wall, he wandered through morning crowds in the main square. He felt too tired to pursue the search but forced himself to ask people—vendors or people with little else to do other than loll about, watching comings and goings—who might know of his friends from Sharvik. No one remembered a large group of strangers or would tell him what they might know. After a year, perhaps Julin and the others were viewed as residents now.

He slipped into an alley where he knew a food vendor usually peddled his wares. With only the one copper, he held off buying food or drink, but his hunger wouldn't let him wait any longer. He bought two small loaves of bread, a small block of cheese, and several strips of lamb on a skewer.

The street was quiet at this hour, most people having eaten earlier, and the vendor was talkative. As Dzorin munched on one of the round loaves, he listened to the middle-aged man complain about his life, with a description of his day thus far.

"Two boys ran by, grabbed a loaf each as they passed," he complained toothlessly. "No way can we leave our stalls to chase the thieves and have more come up behind us, can we? The king's soldiers are never around. If they can't protect us honest sellers, who can?"

Dzorin shook his head and took another bite from the loaf. "Your wife bakes good bread."

"Wife? Not married. Mother used to do the baking, but she died. People moved in a few months ago. Their women make good bread. Two pretty young things bring loaves every morning for me to sell."

Dzorin stopped chewing. "Where did these people come from?" he asked.

"From the east somewhere, I think."

"Where are they now?"

"Stayed together outside the walls. 'Bout a mile east near a stream. Still live in tents."

"Thanks," Dzorin shouted as he took off in the direction of the eastern gate.

The day warmed as he hurried. He passed out of the city and found himself on a narrow road leading toward a large copse of trees, like any other where there was a stream or pool. The trees were farther away than they looked, and the walk took longer than he expected. The prevailing winds were from the west, blowing both city sounds and smells in the same direction, but they were weakened by the distance.

Eventually, those were replaced by sounds from ahead. Dzorin's heart leapt as he entered the wooded area. He approached unseen through the trees, stopping dead when close enough to pick out details.

Never before had he seen such crude living conditions. Makeshift tents were set up here and there among even more makeshift huts built from scrap wood, stones, and tent pieces. Clearly, circumstances had not favored his people after they left Sharvik. Shaking his head, he stepped from between two dwellings into the center of the compound. Eyes devoid of hope watched him move past. No one called a greeting to the warrior returning from the dead, although he recognized many faces, and a few stared with mouths agape. He said nothing, walking silently as if afraid to waken the sleeping souls.

"Dzorin?" a familiar voice shouted in disbelief.

He turned to see Julin, the priest who was his friend for many years, approaching rapidly. He looked no different than when Dzorin last saw him, except his priest's robe was patched and not as clean as usual. Julin held his arms out to embrace him.

"It is truly Dzorin," he said, throwing his arms around the returning warrior.

Dzorin could hardly breathe until Julin finally held him at arm's length. Fearing the priest would pull him into a hug again, he asked questions rapidly, turning Julin to walk beside him.

"How long have you been here? Who is leader now? How do you live? Why does no one greet me but you?"

"We thought you dead, you and Magan. Seeing you in the flesh, strange it seems. No one expected you would come back. Is she with you?"

"No, I left her in Sharvik. We ..."

"Hold, Dzorin. Let me gather the council and some of the priests, and we can tell both tales at once." He led the way to the largest and sturdiest hut. "We meet here. Go in and wait. I will have food sent."

Dzorin shook his head and held up the bread.

"Then have some wine with your bread. I will return soon." He started away but turned back. "We stopped hoping for good news. Only some of the warriors returned."

Before Dzorin could say he did, indeed, have good news, the priest rushed off. Several people stood at a distance, looking as if they'd seen a ghost. He nodded to them; a few nodded back. Others turned away, which was puzzling. He reminded himself they didn't know Iah had been found. He entered the hut, sad at what he saw of his people but knowing his news would make a difference.

Several of the best chairs from the temple of Sharvik stood in a half-circle against the farther wall. He sat facing the door so he could immediately see anyone who entered. Sounds of excited voices came through the opening.

He put the bread in the bag he carried and laid it on the chair next to him, his appetite gone. A woman came in with a cup of wine. He remembered her name was Lorena and having seen her around Sharvik. She watched him warily. He thanked her, and she scuttled back outside.

The wine was bitter, completely unlike what he was accustomed to. Could everything have changed so much?

For months, all he wanted was to find his people, to be among them once more, but events overtook them all, molding lives in ways unforeseen by any of them. These people left their home in Sharvik in despair, certain their god, Iah, was lost to them. In this wood so far from home, they appeared beaten. They were desperate interlopers in an unfamiliar land. No feeling of homecoming rose in his breast as it did on first sighting Sharvik. He found himself pitying these people as if he barely knew them.

Dzorin had not expected such a feeling of isolation, although after the length of time he was apart from them, it shouldn't be surprising. Not to mention, they thought him dead for nearly a year. He suspected many of the scouts sent out to find Iah and bring him back never returned. Surely those who did return had their own adventures to tell, matching those he and Magan experienced.

Once he told the villagers Iah had been found and could be returned, everything would be different. They depended on the god's blessings in ways he no longer could. By leaving Sharvik, they made it clear the god's absence was felt more intensely than he imagined.

On discovering his home abandoned, he found it difficult to believe the people simply walked away, leaving their lives behind so completely. Had his adventures changed him? Of course. Was he the one who no longer belonged because of those changes? Were forces other than the loss of their god responsible for giving up their homes?

Once they returned home, the people he knew so well would come alive, and he could once more be one of them.

People stood inside and outside the hut. The priests sat in their chairs, the village elders stood arrayed behind them. They had drifted in, curious to see the scout they thought dead, yet wary of what he was to tell them.

Dzorin stood in the half-circle, reciting his and Magan's adventures. He paced, facing the villagers, then the leaders. He expressed joy at finding them and described Sharvik, how the buildings were in great condition. The irrigation works needed repair, of course, but could be put right in no time.

He knew where Iah was, and they could retrieve him at any time. "We lost the trail for a time," he said, speaking of the raiders. "Discovered later some sort of magical spell gave them the ability to move without leaving a trace."

He glossed over how, once it was found, they got the heavy idol off of the wagon and into the riverbed. He mentioned nothing of Tarn's challenge or his death. He remembered Vanthi's joining them just before catching up with the raiders and told how he was lost in a flood in a canyon, still a painful memory after the passage of time.

The priests, who seemed to be in charge, asked many questions about the raiders and how they managed to hide their trail. Where was this riverbed where Iah was buried? They wanted to know about his and Magan's time in Mari, but he told them only they were forced to participate in the ceremonies in the arena. Those who managed to get inside murmured amongst themselves; some passed the news to those outside.

When he finished telling them as much as he could in a short time, he looked around the assemblage, waiting for their expressions to change to happiness. All he saw was wariness. No joy. Perhaps suspicion.

Julin, standing among the other priests, began speaking of their loss of hope as months passed. He spoke first of the death of Amleth on the night of the raid, and his not being replaced as high priest. It was easy to infer Julin was looked to for guidance by the people. However, it seemed Garaf assumed leadership of the priests and now this gathering. He spoke little, but Julin showed deference to him as the one everyone believed Amleth chose to be his successor.

Julin told of when it came time for planting, the river flooded at the usual time, but with such force the waters washed away the seedlings in the fields. Many animals were lost. Afterward, the river went down to levels where it impossible to irrigate what was left of the crops. Iah was gone, his blessing the fields not possible.

The journey to the capital, where they all hoped to begin

again, was remembered with horror. Wagons broke down. Much of their supply of water was lost when jugs fell off a wagon and shattered. The heat was intense. Several of the older people died toward the end of their trek, including two of the leading elders. Their numbers so depleted, the council of elders no longer held authority. It sounded as if they turned over all leadership duties to the priests.

Dzorin watched the people's faces as they were reminded of the hardships they endured. Would they be able to endure the reverse trek home? What were the intentions of the priests?

The basic tales told, the priests dismissed everyone, saying they would discuss what to do. Why any discussion was necessary, except to decide when they would leave, was a mystery to Dzorin.

Offers were made for a place to sleep, but Dzorin chose to spread a blanket on the ground a short distance from everyone. There was no one he felt close enough to, except Julin, but the priest shared a tent with two others. He was also more accustomed to sleeping under the stars and for the moment chose not to change.

Julin walked with him until they came to a space the priest thought suitable. A fallen tree nearby provided a seat for the two of them. Julin sat while Dzorin spread his blanket. Everything else was held in a large carpet bag: sword, extra pair of shoes, a length of rope. When he took the knife in its scabbard from his belt, Julin remarked on its beauty.

"I've rarely seen a finer piece."

Dzorin held it up, realizing he was loath to part with it. But it brought bad memories. Perhaps Lahnlee wouldn't accept its return.

Aloud, he said, "It was a gift."

Julin raised an eyebrow but said nothing. Instead, he waited for the warrior to join him on the log.

"What our people have been through, you need to understand," he said. "Our journey here was a difficult one. After everything that happened in Sharvik—the raid, losing Iah, Amleth's death, and the failure of the crops—the will to carry on no one had."

As he spoke, Dzorin noticed how his friend looked older than he remembered. Not a great deal—a bit of grey at the temples, the hairline receded—and the few patches on his robes. He was learning not only time made a difference, but also the trials of the move. The priest slipped into the odd syntax which marked his early days living in one of the cities on the coast.

Julin filled in the gaps of what happened after Dzorin and Magan left Sharvik.

When Iah was lost and the other scouts returned from the search with no idea where the idol was, the people lost all hope. The priests continued to say Iah would return, but after a time, even they stopped believing. The council of elders had tried for a while to support the priests, reminding the people a few scouts were still out there somewhere, doing all they could to bring god home. But the council fell apart as the members argued among themselves over what to do.

After months of hardship and fear, spirits sank low. He described more fully how, when spring came, the Diyala River swept away the tender crops, then fell to an unexpected level. The fields dried up and irrigation ditches filled in with sand. No one entered the temple to pray, not even the priests after a time, and nearly all hope was gone for the return of the remaining scouts. Two representatives sent to Hattushah to ask the king for help returned with word the king's armies were off to the southwest fighting. The royal guard must remain in the city to guard the king, for it was time for the festivals, and he was chief worshiper of the gods.

The festivals! A new spark came into the people. There were gods in the capital. Even Iah, as a lesser god, had a house there, although its presence would not guarantee employment for the priests, who at first were the most reluctant to trust their fortunes to the capital.

From the time the decision was made to move, the priests, led by Garaf, took more and more control into their own hands. Their hold on authority increased during the journey when the two elders died.

When they reached Hattushah, there were no jobs, arable land, or food. There was, of course, no room within the walls of the city for such a large group of people even if they split up into family groups. Determined to stay together, they had searched about for a plot of land within sight of the walls on which to settle.

The elders were introduced to Crosus, a nephew of the king, who would rent them enough land for a village, but the price was crippling: three hundred gold pieces, six donkeys, four bullocks, and two camels each year, to be paid in quarters. With little money, they set out to find ways of paying the price.

The only advantages of the site were the clear waters of the spring and the copse of trees providing shade. The villagers were discouraged from trying to find a site anywhere else around the city. Since most of the land outside the walls belonged either to the king or the temple, with only a few hectares owned by rich merchants and nobles of the king's house, there was little other choice.

Once settled in, the priests of Iah began to spend more and more time with their landlord's men and other priests within the city. Now that the opportunity presented itself, Garaf and his followers were reluctant to go home where they might lose their authority over the villagers. Only a few, led by Julin, argued against their policies, but they were ignored. Julin argued for naming a new high priest as a means of showing the people they still believed in the authority of Iah, but Garaf was not prepared to ignore tradition, even though doing so would help solidify his control. The ritual of naming a high priest could only take place in the presence of Iah, in his own temple, he said. Neither was available.

"Food is somewhat scarce," Julin said. "But we have plenty of bread. The wine ..." He shrugged.

Dzorin told him the bread led him to find them. "A street vendor told me where you were."

They fell silent. The sun was past zenith, the air growing warmer in spite of the shade of the trees. Both men were lost in their own thoughts, incorporating what they were told by the other into their memories. Dzorin was concluding it was Garaf's decisions which brought them all to such a low state.

Julin stood and stretched. "I've work to do. We must get

together to discuss where we go from here."

"Surely it's just a matter of making plans to return to Sharvik."

"Perhaps. I hope so. But the people have changed. As you see," he waved a hand at their surroundings, "none are rushing to talk with you about the village or finding Iah."

"Garaf?"

"He's part of it." Julin turned to leave, stopped and turned back. "Having you return makes me glad." He said. "I can't wait to see Magan."

Dzorin nodded. He couldn't wait to see her either.

CHAPTER 7

Two boys and a girl, all under twelve, stared from a distance. When they realized Dzorin spotted them, they giggled and ran away. He smiled. At least the children showed an interest.

It was early morning, the day after he had reached the encampment. Julin came by with bread and a cup of the sour wine. They made plans to meet with the priests and the remaining elders. Julin spoke to the two remaining elders, but not the priests.

"They will not be happy with my interference," he said and sighed. "They have become used to it, but liking it? No."

After the priest left, Dzorin sat on the log, eating the bread, avoiding the wine. He pulled out the block of cheese he'd purchased the previous morning, making the meal more palatable. He finished, washed everything down with water from his waterskin, and re-wrapped the remains. He was putting it all into his carpet bag when he heard footsteps behind him.

He grabbed hold of the knife, nearest to his hand, when a familiar voice spoke. "It's me, Dzorin. Sher."

He let the knife slide back into the bag and turned. Sher stood grinning behind him with Varas, their captain, at his side. Varas wasn't smiling, but he rarely did.

"We wanted to welcome you back," Varas said. "Such as it is. We should have come over yesterday, but ... we haven't come to grips with everything, truth to tell. Especially the news you and Magan found Iah."

"How many of us did we lose?" Dzorin asked.

"Five of those who went in search," Varas said. "Not including you and Magan, of course. We were sure the two of you were dead."

"Came close a couple of times."

Varas nodded. "I'm guessing you didn't tell half of what happened yesterday."

"No." Dzorin smiled. "It was quite an adventure."

"Magan is well?" Sher asked. He was her best friend among the warriors.

"Yes, when we parted."

At Dzorin's invitation, they all sat down, Sher and Varas on the log, Dzorin on his blanket. After exchanging a few more pleasantries, Dzorin asked, "How do the warriors feel about returning to Sharvik?"

"We're all for it," Sher said. Varas nodded agreement. "We have no role here. We're not really needed. But that isn't it. We see our people disintegrating before our eyes. They also have little purpose here."

"But?"

Varas frowned. "The priests are doing very well in the city. It's pretty clear they prefer to stay and hobnob with the other priests and high officials. They are working on taking over Iah's temple here. The current residents are old. Apparently Iah isn't one of the most popular gods in the city, but in the past few months, they have managed to bring him into better—and more lucrative—repute."

"Garaf and the others are getting rich in other words."

"Very. Maybe you'll get to see their tents." Varas shook his head. "It's a shame. Most of the people live in horrible conditions, and the priests eat well and have luxurious surroundings. All except Julin and the two who follow him."

Dzorin saw enough of conditions in the camp to suspect this was true. As a former acolyte, he knew firsthand how the priests used their positions to get the best of everything. Back in Sharvik, it wasn't too terrible a thing since conditions were good for everyone. Now, the people needed all the support they could get. It wasn't surprising Garaf would take advantage of them and their current situation.

"How hard will the priests fight to stay?"

"Garaf will block us all the way. If the people return to Sharvik, he might just stay here."

"The other priests probably will be divided," Sher added. "They aren't reaping all of the same benefits by being here. If Garaf and his closest supporters decide to stay, there will be higher positions for others back home."

"It's the people we must convince then. I doubt we could talk Garaf into willingly giving up all of the benefits he's getting here."

"Julin will be our biggest help," Sher said. "The people believe in him. Some are afraid of Garaf."

They probably have reason to be, Dzorin thought. The high priest was never a friend to him, and he was downright bitter toward Magan.

They set about planning how to proceed. There were two issues to be settled: how to convince everyone to return to Sharvik, and once that was done, how to move everyone back without their suffering as much as they did nearly a year ago.

Over the next few days, Dzorin and Julin met publicly with the high priest and his advisors. Privately, they met with villagers in small groups. At first, everyone was reluctant to pack up and move again. The people admitted conditions weren't wonderful there, outside Hattushah. The priests thought things were great and it wasn't worth anyone's time and effort to move.

More and more, a few wanted very much to return home. This large city wasn't home. It was all right for a while, but that time was over. They were farmers, not merchants, and their land had lain fallow for over a year. It was time to repair the irrigation system and re-plant the crops. They in turn spoke to others and their numbers grew. There was a longing for the simpler life at home. Although, Dzorin knew, if they were honest with themselves, that life could also be very hard. But he wasn't going to remind them, especially since it was true they were all healthier and happier before.

A small fire burned low in the center of the space he occupied and he, Julin, Varas, and Sher sat around it, discussing plans for the journey to come. It wasn't going to be easy, and after suffering through the earlier trek, the people were more likely to give up easily. Once they reached the point of no return, those who objected might become more amenable.

However, they hoped by planning everything out carefully, most problems would be avoided. Tonight, they discussed equipment and supplies.

Water jugs must be replaced. Parts for the wagons that weren't used since they arrived had to be found. Some required a near rebuilding because part of the wood was used to construct huts and support tents. Harness needed repair for the bullocks which pulled the wagons.

Loaves of bread could be sold to bring in some of the money needed, and more to take with them. How else to get enough to buy the things they could not make? Some personal items, anything they no longer used, could be sold. Everyone who worked inside the city walls would be asked to pool their wages.

Things such as charcoal, food, salt, anything perishable, must also be purchased. They'd already determined there was plenty of rope to secure items and material to use as covers, and they had makeshift tents.

They not only had to supply everything for the journey, they also must gather enough food and other supplies for the first couple of months in Sharvik. If they left Hattushah on time, they would arrive in Sharvik in early spring. The floods would come, the soil would be ready, and crops would be planted.

"We may not have to take everything," Julin said.

The others looked at him curiously.

"We did try to plan ahead," he said. "Before we left, we buried dried beans and lentils in clay pots in several locations."

"Magan and I found a couple of those," Dzorin said. "We had no idea there was more, although we should have suspected."

"You found the ones we left in your home?"

"Yes."

"Some of us thought … well, you know."

Dzorin nodded.

"There are many more, some in the granary, others in separate dwellings. It was the one thing we possessed in great supply. There will be enough for a couple of weeks. Maybe a month."

It was good news. Just as they were about to congratulate Julin for his foresight, a figure stepped into the circle of light.

"Celebrating something?"

The voice was recognizable to all. Garaf, followed by two of those he called his advisors were paying them a visit. A sense of foreboding swept over Dzorin.

"May we join you?"

"Of course," Dzorin said.

Dzorin stared as one of the followers unfolded a wooden stool for the high priest to sit on. He and the other follower stood behind him, arms folded into the sleeves of their robes. Garaf looked around the group and smiled at the four of them.

"Now, how may I help?"

"With what, my lord?" Julin asked.

"With your plans. I assume you are discussing the return to Sharvik and how it can be accomplished."

"Discussing only," Julin said. The others watched Garaf. Dzorin wondered why the high priest was there.

"There is much to plan for, we all know. I and the priests who follow me," he looked meaningfully at Julin, "are ready to do what we can. Within reason."

"Which means?" Dzorin spoke up.

"I visited with Lord Crosus today. It seems he is not pleased with the idea of your leaving precipitously and without honoring the contract for the lease of the land. There are still six months to go and he intends holding you to the agreement."

Julin and Dzorin exchanged a glance. Garaf's calling it "your leaving" held serious implications. Among the plans already discussed, paying extra in hopes of making it easier for Lord Crosus to accept their leaving in time for the spring floods, was one of the most worrisome. It was important they arrive in Sharvik in time for planting.

"And he renewed his petition for Ileana to join his harem. He has every intention of winning her over." Garaf said this with self-satisfaction.

Dzorin frowned. He had not heard of this complication.

"I'm certain we can work all of this out and we can plan to leave in six, perhaps nine months from now. There is no real need to hurry, is there?"

"If we don't leave soon, we will miss the spring floods,"

Dzorin said. "We could also lose the people's willingness to return."

"That would not be such a bad thing, surely. Life here is different than in the village, but we have made ourselves welcome and manage to survive. We kept warm in the winter. The women's bread is very popular in the city. We have clean water and shelter."

"The people are farmers," Dzorin said. "They aren't merchants nor do many practice other professions. The spirits of our people yearn to be home. Raising their own crops and animals. Hunting and fishing. Worshiping in their own temple."

"But not this year. Crosus will not let us break the contract. I'm afraid we will have to wait. Besides, how certain are you the people truly want to return? What makes you such a good judge of their needs? Is it more your own need? Are you trying to convince them what is best for them?"

Garaf stood. "The question is moot, of course. We cannot leave until Lord Crosus releases us from the contract."

His man folded the stool and the three walked away into the darkness. The four watched them disappear, leaving them to their own doubts.

"No one mentioned Ileana and Crosus's interest in her before," Dzorin said.

"We thought he was over her," Julin said. "Lord Crosus saw her in the city one day when she delivered bread to his kitchens. Afterward, he followed her whenever he saw her. He eventually approached her, she said no. He talked to the elders, they said it was her decision. Then he talked with Garaf. Crosus went away and no one knows what was said, but we all assumed it was over."

"If It's a big obstacle to our leaving, perhaps Ileana could be persuaded to change her mind," Sher said. "Convince her to stay so he will cancel the contract."

"If she were your sister or daughter, would you ask her to sacrifice herself?" Julin said.

"I don't know," Sher said. "For the sake of all our people, I might."

Julin shook his head. "Our women aren't to be bargained away. It's her decision."

Dzorin agreed with Julin, but at the same time understood Sher's point. He would never try to convince Ileana to accept Crosus's proposal, much less force her to do so. But he decided to speak with her to determine her feelings on the matter for himself.

The positive mood that had prevailed over the four before Garaf appeared was gone. They said goodnight, and Dzorin was left staring into the fire. Was Garaf right? Returning to Sharvik was his dream and no one else's?

He and Magan fought so hard to get back. It was what kept them going over the year which followed the raid on Sharvik. The villagers and Iah returning was the only possible outcome of everything that happened. How could he give it up after struggling so hard?

No matter what happened, he had to get back to Sharvik and Magan. Even if it meant only the two of them lived in the village, which was ridiculous. Maybe they would go out on their own, visit other places, see how others lived.

He lay down on the blanket, memories shifting through his mind. His last thought before falling asleep: We must return. All of us.

CHAPTER 8

Next morning, Sher appeared with a loaf of bread and small jug of wine. He joined Dzorin on the log and handed the bread to his friend. The two munched on the last of Dzorin's cheese. When Dzorin declined the wine, Sher said, "This isn't the bad stuff. I get my own in the city."

A sip proved he was right and Dzorin accepted a half-full cup.

"You've had quite an adventure," Sher said.

"No more than you, I think."

Sher nodded. He handed the loaf back to his friend. "Magan stayed behind in Sharvik, you said."

"Yes, at least I left her there. She was going to … she went on another quest."

"She always was an odd one."

Dzorin nodded. He hoped Sher wasn't going to say anything derogatory about their fellow warrior. He and Magan were friends for many years, but as a whole, the warriors were never comfortable having a woman among them.

"She'll be in the village when we get back," Dzorin said, hoping it was true. They'd learned how anything could happen during their travels.

"I look forward to seeing her." They were silent a moment, then Sher said, "The captain is calling the warriors together to train and practice. We've not stopped the whole time here, but not like we did in Sharvik."

He added more wine to Dzorin's cup. He savored the taste, especially after the vinegary taste of the other that hit the back of his throat and made him shiver.

"It's a long way for such a large group of people. When we left the village, it was … well, let's just say it wasn't well planned. The priests were against it at the time. I suspect they were afraid they would lose authority in the city. Turns out they were wrong, though. They've allied with Crosus and other priests as we said. They have power in the city they never experienced in Sharvik."

"We will have to work together," Dzorin said. "Everyone. Hopefully we've all learned from the mistakes of the past."

Sher nodded and began asking questions about the other's adventures. They'd had little time alone, and Dzorin realized he was very interested in how Magan was, how she did on their trek, whether the two of them got along. "When you didn't return, everyone was certain you were both dead. There wasn't time to mourn. The elders began urging us to leave."

"How many of the others managed to get back?" He asked earlier but hadn't gotten an answer.

"Cail and I, of course. Leod and Hein, Dered, Bech, Varas came back without Murra, and Isik without Vanthi."

"Isik made it back?" He had yet to see all of his fellow warriors, unsure about how they would receive him and how he would feel about becoming one of them again.

"Yes. He barely made it before we moved. He was banged up pretty badly. Too bad about Vanthi."

"Yes. He wasn't sure Isik would make it back, but he thought his duty was to keep after Iah."

"Ironic in a way."

Dzorin nodded. Looking up, he saw the sun well above the horizon. The two warriors sat in companionable silence, taking sips of wine now and then. They reminisced for a while and talked about how best to move the villagers back east to Sharvik. "I'm sure Varas and Garaf will figure things out. I know Garaf doesn't want to leave, but he'll come around when we need him."

"We'll see. He seems pretty happy with things the way they are."

Sher shook his head. "He doesn't talk to many people. I'm sure he doesn't confide in Julin, anymore."

They ate their fill and stoppered the wine jug. Dzorin shook out the blanket and rolled up his things in it, except for the bronze sword he wore across his back most of the time. He debated whether to take the knife. He didn't expect anyone to rifle through his things, but he wouldn't risk losing it. As usual, he stuck it in his belt under the tunic, not wanting to explain how he came by it.

They went looking for Julin and Varas to plan for the day's activities. Dzorin pushed aside his doubts from the night before. He'd seen too clearly how the people were when he arrived—tired, unhappy—and he was certain many, if not all, wanted to return home. With the support of his friends, he would help them do just that.

They found Varas drilling the warriors. None of them complained. Instead, they seemed to welcome the new feeling of purpose. The captain nodded to the two of them, and they joined in the exercises. Dzorin realized it had been much too long since he'd worked on toning his muscles and was surprised at how tough it was. He persevered, knowing they would all need every bit of strength and tenacity they could muster.

He didn't doubt Crosus could make everything difficult for them. The landlord needed to be convinced to let them leave, and it was clear Garaf would be of little help there.

Thinking of Crosus reminded him of the young woman, Ileana. It was time to talk with her, see what her feelings were. After Varas dismissed them, Dzorin asked Julin to introduce him to her. They found her at the well, drawing water.

"Ileana," Julin said, "this is Dzorin. A word with you he wants."

From the phraseology, Dzorin knew the priest was nervous about what he might say to the young woman. On his part, Dzorin understood why Crosus might be enamored with her.

He remembered her as a beautiful young girl. She was still both beautiful and young. He also remembered Sher was attracted to her at one time but acknowledged she was too young for marriage and too young for him. Dzorin wasn't certain how many years were between their ages, but she now appeared old enough to make such a decision on her own. Surprising how much a year could change things.

He asked Julin to stay while he talked with her to avoid any appearance of impropriety, but to say nothing. The two men walked with Ileana as she carried the water jug to her tent.

"Where is your father?" Julin asked.

"He has gone into the city. He needed some supplies. He's begun making jewelry again." Her smile expressed how happy that made her better than any words could.

The priest reminded Dzorin that Lugal was the goldsmith in Sharvik and once they left the village, he stopped working. "His heart isn't in it anymore." It would seem the prospect of returning home lifted his spirits.

She set the jug down on a rickety table, motioned for the two men to sit on a narrow bench and sat on a small stool. Her expression changed from apprehension and curiosity and back again.

"Julin has told me about Crosus's proposal to you," Dzorin began. Ileana straightened and her eyes widened. He raised his hand, palm toward her. "I'm not here to try to convince you to accept him," he said. "It's only some are convinced if you did, he would let all of us go home without interference."

She shook her head. Her hands gripped the edges of the small stool she sat on. "I can't. I won't."

"Does he frighten you?"

She nodded.

"Has he said anything, threatened you or anyone else?"

She looked uncomfortable, reluctant to speak. Glancing at Julin, her eyes pleaded.

"It's all right, child," Julin said. "Dzorin only wants to understand what has happened."

She nodded and looked back to the warrior. Looking him in the eye, she spoke.

"Once when I was in the city, we met, whether by accident or intentionally, I don't know. He repeated his proposal. When I shook my head, he grabbed my wrist. 'I could take you right here on the street if I wanted.' Two of his guardsmen were behind him. I was with my friend, but she couldn't do anything to help."

She took a deep breath.

"I didn't think I would ever be able to come back here. He's so old and his breath stinks."

Julin coughed and Dzorin guessed his friend might be the same age as the landlord. That would make Crosus nearly fifty.

When he focused back on Ileana, tears streaked down her cheeks. No doubt, she was afraid of the man.

"No one will force you to accept his proposal," he said. "I needed to know how things stood." He reached over and patted her hand lying in her lap. "Don't be afraid. And don't go into the city again. You should be safe here."

She grabbed his hand and squeezed it. "Thank you," she said.

Over the next few days, the warriors trained and got their weapons back in shape. More than the usual number of loaves of bread were baked to sell in the city so they could buy things they needed for the journey. They sold as many of their possessions as they could spare, including a worn-out wagon and a few of the animals. Lugal worked on carving small religious figures out of stone and wood to sell in the market. There wasn't much else besides a few pieces of jewelry which brought a decent price.

Several of the younger women entered the temple brothels soon after arriving in Hattushah to raise money for the rent. They'd also saved quite a bit which they gave to their relatives and friends to buy supplies and tools for the trek home. Their generosity made it possible to purchase much of what was needed. Being exotic with their light brown hair, unlike the usual black hair of women in the city, they were popular and earned good money. Some of the money they made was used to buy flour with which the other women made the bread sold to the street vendors and wealthy households. Thus, they made two quarterly payments.

The third quarter was about to begin. The hope was to raise enough money to pay the entire third quarter rent in hopes Crosus would be satisfied.

"It has been full of difficulties, our life here," Julin said one evening as they ate, "but we have survived. Soon we will begin again."

As the days passed, Julin and all of the warriors moved among the people, talking about their return to Sharvik, especially since Iah would soon be back in his temple. Once over the shock of Dzorin's return, many wanted to hear of his and Magan's adventures. He emphasized her role in the rescue, knowing many of their fellow villagers were always suspicious of her, a woman warrior, not fitting into what was considered the normal role for a person of her gender. He realized, as he talked with others, many were still suspicious of her because of rumors that spread about her being a witch.

He noticed, too, Ileana began hanging around, listening in on the conversations, bringing him a cup of water or wine. She disappeared when he was among his fellow warriors, though. When he was alone or talking with Julin or Sher, he would spot her nearby, pretending to be on some errand or another. He spoke to the priest about it.

"She probably feels safer when she has you in sight. There are still some who would have her give herself to Crosus to make their lives easier."

Dzorin nodded and pushed the distraction of the girl from his mind to concentrate on the plans for their departure. Overall relief began to set in as their plans came together. Not everyone was excited about getting back to Sharvik, and there would be some staying behind. When asked, those thinking of staying were not sure what they would do or where they would live. They wouldn't be able to afford the rent on the grove, of course. But the majority looked forward to returning to their old lives, to farming, and everything else familiar. The more they discussed their return, the higher their spirits rose.

"The hardships they've experienced the past year makes it difficult for some," Julin said behind him as the two walked to the well.

"Surely it means everyone is happy about the news I bring. Wasn't it the loss of Iah that brought those hardships? Now, they can return to the lives they knew."

It was difficult for him to understand how the villagers

wouldn't be excited and eager about returning home. His own enthusiasm only increased because of the lack of eagerness in others. Overall, though, they were changing, as more and more villagers worked hard to make their return a reality.

"It will take more than words to lift some from their lethargy. Despair has dogged them over the months since Iah was taken. Life here wasn't what they expected. The hopes they carried from Sharvik were dashed."

Dzorin started to remind the priest he and Magan suffered over those months. He wanted to say again, Iah was found and could be back in Sharvik very soon. But the people must act.

"We need to be certain enough of them go with us to bring the village back to life," he said, instead. "If too many remain here, the village may still die."

"Give them time. Realization is coming. I've seen more hope in them than they've felt in a very long time."

Dzorin smiled at Julin's optimism. "I'll leave giving them the will to you."

They reached the well. Dzorin pulled the rope raising the large gourd filled with water. He poured some over his head to cool off and handed the gourd to Julin who drank deeply. Dzorin rubbed his face with his hands. When he opened his eyes, Ileana stood close, holding a cloth for him to dry off. He took it, thanked her, and exchanged a glance with Julin. From his expression, it appeared the priest might now understand his apprehensions.

Julin blessed him and wandered back toward the center of the camp. Dzorin thanked the girl and made his way to the edge of the grove to spread his blanket. He sorted through the items he kept wrapped up during the day. He pulled the knife Lahnlee gave him from under his belt. The sun was low to the west and if he held it a certain way, the jewels in the scabbard reflected the light. It was beautiful. He was still loath to part with it but felt there was no choice. He would have to return to the inn and tell the merchant the whole story of his son Tarn's death. And return the knife. After three weeks though, would he still be there?

Ileana approached, offering bread and cheese. He took them

and set them on his blanket. "Ileana, we have to talk."

Her eyes widened in anticipation. Before he could continue, Sher appeared, his footsteps crunching softly in the sand. "Time to patrol," he said, raising an eyebrow toward the girl.

Varas set a schedule for the warriors to patrol the perimeter in pairs.

Ileana hurried away. Dzorin took a deep breath and let it out. "I think she's formed a crush on me."

"It would seem so," Sher said. "And you?"

"I'm pledged to Magan." He realized this was the first time he'd uttered those words.

Sher's eyebrows shot upward. "Ah. Be careful, my friend."

"I know. Ileana's so young. I don't want to hurt her."

"You may have to."

He stood, wondering at the same time if Sher was still attracted to the young girl, now a young woman. He turned away and thrust the knife back into his belt, still not wanting to answer any questions about where he got it. He couldn't tell the truth and he wouldn't lie.

The grove was large, and people were spread out over the entire area, although from a short distance away, a visitor would not have known there were so many living there. They moved about, leaving the tents of friends or family after eating, some strolling arm in arm in the soft twilight. People greeted them as they passed. One older man clapped Dzorin on the shoulder. "Thought you were dead," he said with a chuckle. It was surprising he still got that reaction sometimes.

Living conditions were poor for all he saw, some more than others. Was it possible many things were the same as in Sharvik and only the setting made them seem poorer? That and the richness of the priests' dwellings, which he'd decided not to visit. From a distance, the opulence was obvious. It seemed the people didn't notice; perhaps enough time passed for their richness to become part of daily life, overlooked and unenvied.

They completed the circuit just as darkness fell. They reported to Varas all was quiet. Two more warriors set out on night patrol, nodding as they passed each other. Sher walked back with Dzorin to where he slept on the blanket spread on the ground.

"Are you still comfortable here?" Sher asked. "We can make room for you with the rest of us."

For a moment, being among the other warriors seemed a good idea. If nothing else, it would discourage Ileana from appearing as she had earlier. But the idea of being crowded into a tent with the others didn't appeal to him.

"It's fine. I've grown quite accustomed to sleeping on the ground."

"I'll at least get another blanket." Sher left without waiting for his consent. Returning a short time later, he tossed the wool blanket to him.

"Thanks."

"See you tomorrow." Sher turned away then back. "Welcome back," he said. "I don't think I said that before."

"I know. Soon we all can say, 'Welcome home.'"

They bid each other good night. Sher walked away toward the center of the camp, his silhouette moving against the light of a distant fire.

Dzorin lay down but could not sleep. Distant conversations came softly to his ear. A dog barked, became quiet. Their little settlement was never utterly silent.

His people weren't so beaten down they didn't care about the future. He, Sher, Julin, and whoever else could raise their own good cheer and would work on the rest. A difficult time lay ahead, and if they weren't ready when they needed to be, it would be even harder, especially if Garaf opposed them openly.

He lay on his back, hands behind his head, looking at the stars blinking between tree limbs. His thoughts turned to Magan. He missed her lying beside him, hearing her voice, her breathing as she slept. Did she find the teacher she sought? He hoped so. Even so, he wished she had left with him. Her help would be so appreciated over the next weeks. He missed her support and strength. Life without her wasn't as exciting.

CHAPTER 9

"The distance is too far, the journey too hard."

Joel, a villager Dzorin never met before, voiced his fear and reluctance to make the journey home to Sharvik. Julin and he were visiting with families who expressed reluctance to return, reminding them of their former lives and how Iah would soon join them. As farmers, most of the people were accustomed to hard work but for some, repeating the hardships of the months of travel was too much.

Dzorin spoke, instead, of the hardships and deaths of those who went out to find their stolen god. He described the months in which he and Magan fought to return with the news Iah was no longer in the hands of the raiders. He spoke of Vanthi's death in the flash flood, his voice catching as he described the search but never finding his body. In describing Magan's trials, he did not mention the magic with which she defeated Friya, the sorceress and high priestess of Mari.

"Magan waits for us even now within the walls of Sharvik. She is ready to return to the riverbed and fetch Iah home."

Everyone listened, many expressed sympathy, even wonder, at the escapes and struggles. A few were convinced returning to Sharvik was their reward for the suffering of them all. Others were not so easily swayed. Still, the two of them, the warrior and the priest, talked and more agreed to return.

Except this day. Joel remained intractable, not surprising since he lost his eldest child in the journey to Hattushah.

Once Julin felt they had done all they could, they left Joel alone, wishing him well if he did, indeed, stay behind. Dzorin went to his own little camp. Once more, he pulled the knife from the bundle. It was time to face Lahnlee. The merchant needed to know how his son died and where he was buried.

Before he started toward the city, he heard running footsteps behind. Turning, he saw Ileana stop just short of him.

"You are going into the city?"

"Yes."

"Take me with you. I haven't been there since ..."

"You shouldn't be seen there. If Lord Crosus sees you it will only cause trouble."

"Yes, but ..."

"Go back, Ileana. Don't make things harder on yourself."

Her shoulders slumped and her smile dropped into a pout.

"I'll be back soon." He waited for her to retrace her steps. "Go on. I'm not going to be long."

She walked slowly, dragging her feet, and looked back once.

Dzorin took a deep breath and exhaled slowly. Julin agreed she might be besotted with "the warrior who promised to protect her." as he phrased it. She was a lovely, sweet girl, and they both hoped it wouldn't become a problem.

Finding the inn wasn't difficult. Dzorin took a chair at one of the tables in the tavern. Six weeks had passed since he was last there, but nothing seemed to have changed at all. The same men, or their lookalikes, sat at the same table in the gloomy darkness of the far corner. The sour smell of bad wine and food hung in the air. The only difference was the absence of Lahnlee across the table.

The serving girl appeared as before. A hint of recognition touched her eyes as she approached.

"I'm looking for Lahnlee, the man with the broken leg I brought here for lodging."

She shook her head.

"The landlord and I carried his belongings to a room on the second floor."

"He left."

"Left? When?"

"After three days."

"How? He wasn't able to walk by himself."

"He hired some men and some camels." She turned away satisfied the conversation was at an end.

"Do you know which way he went? Did he stay in the city?"

"Wine?" she asked.

He shook his head. He had no money, and he wanted to return to the village. There was so much work to do for the return to Sharvik. "Please. Did he leave the city?"

She regarded him for a moment. "Yes," she said and disappeared through the doorway in the back.

Dzorin sat puzzling over the merchant's leaving. Lahnlee had planned on staying in the city for a time, his stated reason being to continue the search for his son. That was no longer necessary. Dzorin told Lahnlee he would come back with information on the location of Tarn's body, but he'd gotten so busy, too much so to justify taking the time away from the camp. He was of two minds about facing the merchant and delayed too long.

With much trepidation but determined to do what he thought was the right thing, he returned to tell Lahnlee the details of what happened to his son. He was also prepared to take him to the burial spot if Lahnlee wanted or bring the body to the father. But the merchant hadn't even waited several days. A week could be a very long time to sit and wait.

He should feel guilty, himself, about waiting too long, but could do nothing about it now. Although he knew where Lahnlee came from, it would be a very long time before a journey there could be made. He stood and walked back into the afternoon sunshine. It would be nice to think this problem was over and the only things to worry about were his people and their god. If only the feelings of guilt over the death of Tarn would simply go away. He wasn't the one who sliced the raider's throat, yet his life was saved when Magan made it happen by turning Tarn's own sword against him.

In his mind's eye, he saw Tarn's sword turn, the edge of the blade slice across the man's throat, his blood spilling onto the sand. The three of them—Magan, Vanthi, and himself—pushing and pulling the body into the hole. The golden idol lay on its back, the warrior beside it on his side as if the two were lovers.

If they had buried them well, both were still there, waiting for him and Magan to return. After the events of the past year, he didn't believe it would be easy.

It wasn't until he met the raider's father he felt guilt about killing the raider. It was a warrior's lot to face death, his own or the enemy's. But getting to know the father turned Tarn into a real person, although Dzorin knew if it all happened again, he would not hesitate to kill.

Returning to the village, he found everyone about their tasks with more spirit. Julin moved from group to group, raising their outlook on the future, reminding them of life in the village, their homes. They were going home and Iah would be returned to them. Life would be as it was before the raiders stole their god. Julin made no great speeches but continued speaking with individuals, families, and groups to encourage them, remind them of what was good about their lives before coming to the capital.

Dzorin, his own mood lightened by the enthusiasm of his friend, joined Captain Varas, Julin, and other leaders, discussing the conditions in Sharvik as they were when he left the empty village. The irrigation system, damaged but not in ruins. Dust and dirt lay everywhere. Roofs needed patching. The main gates were in good order, at least, as were the buildings.

They planned the return journey, deferring somewhat to Dzorin, who more recently traversed the same ground. He also spoke of retrieving Iah, where he was buried, how he and Magan could lead them back to the riverbed. He was asked again about her, why she didn't come with him to Hattushah, but he gave a vague response, saying only she had another quest.

At night he lay on his blanket on the ground, missing the warmth of her body beside him. Was she well? Was she working too hard with the teacher he hoped she'd found?

In the final days, when a delegation was sent to Lord Crosus to inform him of their impending departure, the landowner expressed his displeasure. He emphasized his disapproval of the prospect of losing tenants, sending word with Garaf. He reminded them their lease was not expired and told them they would have to wait until he consulted the priests in the temple of Dagan, to whom part of the rent money was paid. The villagers offered an extra month's rent, hoping he would relent. Crosus sent them away without an answer.

Dzorin was not prepared to wait any longer than necessary, nor were many others once their longing for home was reignited. More than a year had passed since the raid on Sharvik; it was time to return. They didn't want to wait to reclaim their lost way of life, and they worked long hours to get everything ready.

"Is the money so important to him?" Dzorin asked the others as they discussed the landlord. "He's already very rich."

"It is the most important thing to him," Julin said. "He lives a life of indulgence. However, his desire for Ileana also drives him. He has petitioned the elders and the priests to approach her on his behalf. He offered money to her and to us hoping we would turn her over to him."

"There isn't anything we can offer in her place?" Dzorin asked.

Julin looked at the others and cleared his throat. "He is a man with singleness of purpose. We informed him we would not make her go to him, nor would we try to convince her. Although, I think Garaf did speak to her about it. He would do anything Crosus asks in order to stay in his good graces."

"You believe Crosus would try to keep us here because of his lust for her?"

"Oh, yes. To keep her from leaving and to punish us for refusing to just turn her over to him. He would lose face if he doesn't get what he wants. When Crosus or his minions visit, we are careful to hide her away so she can't be seen."

"Why would a man want a woman who didn't want him?"

"He is the uncle of the king and brother of the high priest. No one refuses him anything."

Countering this obstacle appeared impossible, although one of the few people who knew of the predicament suggested they offer the woman in place of the rent money, echoing Garaf's thoughts on the situation. That option was rejected by the rest, so they made plans without taking Ileana into account, except knowing it was a problem. Each day they continued talking to the people, trying to change more minds, and reinforcing the determination of those who decided they would return to Sharvik.

Not many refused to be moved as Joel did. Some were fond of the city and its more exciting way of life. Their skills and wares were popular and sold well. No one looked forward to moving again. They only wanted to be back in their own homes. Enthusiasm grew to the point it filled the camp. The people laughed and moved with more alacrity. The work went faster, and one could see the pride each person took in what they accomplished. Yet, there were still questions.

"How can you be sure Iah is still in that hole? You've been gone a very long time," Oltor, one of Garaf's supporters said one day from a short distance. Two of the elders, Dzorin, Julin, and Varas were meeting with two other men, discussing the order of march. One or another of the priests had taken to following them, listening to what they said to the people, then offering objections. The high priest sent them, of course, although he denied it, saying they only expressed their own doubts.

"We buried him deeply in the sand," Dzorin responded. "It would take months for nature to uncover him, and no man would have reason to dig in the same spot."

Although he was tired of the priests sowing doubts among the villagers, he wasn't without his own doubts. What if he *isn't* still there? What if the riverbed filled with water from the last rainy season in the mountains and the runoff exposed the treasure? The rainy season was due again in a few months, another reason to get back before it happened.

Dzorin forced back the doubts. This was no time for hesitation. His faith in their future must remain strong or his people would never move from this spot. It was he who brought them hope. He who said returning could be done. Left here, they would die or become so assimilated in the city, no one would know they were from Sharvik.

They decided the exit would happen under cover of darkness, three days after the date they told Lord Crosus. He should be caught by surprise, letting him believe they changed their minds, if they could keep Garaf from knowing or telling the landlord. Preparations proceeded rapidly. The people became more eager and some more apprehensive as the day came closer. Once those who were undecided realized most of the people would be leaving, they began changing their minds about staying.

Two women, one a not-so-young widow, the other never married, were not going. They met men in the city who wanted to marry them, they said. Three more women just refused to go, giving no explanation.

"They are the ones who ... um ... worked in the temple," Julin explained later. "As temple prostitutes." He shrugged. "It was what they could do to help earn money and food."

"They can still return with us," Dzorin said. He remembered Julin saying before how much the money they earned to help pay the rent. "Surely the people would not ostracize them after they did all they could to help."

Julin shook his head. "It is an acceptable profession in the city, but our people would not accept them. It was very brave of them," he added, "but they knew the consequences."

In large cities like Hattushah, prostitution was a common practice, accepted by everyone as a fact of life. The women plied their trade in the temples and were looked on as servants of the gods. While not honored, they were not condemned. For people who lived in a small village, however, it was shameful. Although their sacrifice helped to feed everyone, these women would carry this shame with them if they returned to Sharvik. Staying in the capital, their way of life would be more acceptable. They might eventually find husbands if it was what they desired.

Dzorin sighed. He couldn't help but honor these women who sacrificed so much to help their people. Still, it was a problem beyond his abilities to solve. The women made their own choice. For now, he must help bring strength of will to his people, enough to get them home where they could start again.

Julin, remained the most excited about returning home. He carried a spark that flamed when told in the first council meeting Iah was safe and hidden. They need only retrieve him, he reminded everyone, bring him back to Sharvik, and everything would be as it was before.

Dzorin smiled at his exuberance, hoping the priest was right. He had his own reasons for looking forward to returning. Back at Sharvik, he would see Magan again. He preferred not to give anyone details about her staying behind since he could not totally understand her need himself. The villagers never approved of magic or those who practiced it, except in the temple and as practiced by the priests. She hid her abilities as much as she could, but over the years, many guessed she was gifted. He told them she too had survived and how heroic she was in finding Iah. She knew the location of Iah's burial. She and Dzorin together could easily retrace the trail leading to the dry riverbed. He was sure he could find the way alone, but if something happened to him, there was another who could lead the way.

Julin took charge of organizing the packing for the exodus, leaving the planning for security to Dzorin and Captain Varas. They all worked on the order of the march, deciding to place the priests, including Garaf, at the head where they could keep an eye on them.

Several people argued against leaving extra money in the hands of the landowner since the money would buy many things they needed for the long trek. However, when Lord Crosus's collector came for the regular payment, he was given what money they agreed on earlier. Several warriors stood behind him, looking over the camp.

"You plan to leave, I understand," the collector said, as if he'd just learned of their plans. "His Lordship isn't happy about this. He expects a year's notice."

"We informed His Lordship," Julin said. "You have the extra rent money in your hand as agreed upon."

"He is not pleased." The collector looked around at the group of people gathered around them. "He wishes me to speak with the woman, Ileana, to ensure she leaves of her own free will."

"She is busy."

"Still, I cannot leave …"

"She is well," Julin said when the collector didn't continue. "Her modesty must be accepted."

The man frowned, turned abruptly, and climbed onto the

chariot which brought him out of the city. He headed back to the capital, the guards trotting behind.

"We must leave quickly and quietly," Dzorin said. "Otherwise, we may not be able to protect her. Or ourselves."

Preparations proceeded a little faster. Arguments on exactly when they should leave became more urgent.

A few more coins came in during the final days of decision and packing and were used to buy one more wagon and the ox to pull it. Once loaded, little room was left on the wagons or the pack animals for people to ride. If they were lucky, everyone would stay strong and healthy so they could walk.

The day they told the landlord they would leave came and went. In the distance, soldiers could be seen watching them. Everyone went about their usual business to all appearances. By the morning of actual departure three days later, the guards were not there. It appeared the ruse was successful; however, the departure still took place a full day later in the early morning hours. Fires were left burning and shells of the huts still stood. Those who were staying moved around, visible to anyone who might be watching.

In spite of the sure knowledge of hardships lying ahead, the people spoke excitedly of going home. They marched out in good order. Dzorin's own hope returned. Surely, it was time for the gods to favor the people of Sharvik.

The order of march was reviewed many times, and each family and group knew their places, which most took quietly. Some confusion erupted here and there and was dealt with. Few had slept since sundown due to last minute arrangements or anticipating the trek.

Ileana begged to be allowed to walk with Dzorin, but he refused. Her place was with her father and he needed to be free to roam as needed.

Home. Nearly everyone was excited by the prospect of moving back, of living within the walls of the village they knew and loved. Some expressed doubts everything would be as it was before, for good or ill. Doubts and the memory of their difficult journey to the capital were pushed aside.

Those staying behind, stood at the edge of the copse of

trees. A few waved as the caravan moved out. Looking over the long ragtag line, Dzorin questioned the reality of returning to their homes for the last time. He saw the changes in the village's nature brought about after the people left it empty of life. Three or four more months—which was how long he expected for the return trip—would bring about more changes. Were the people ready and able to cope with those changes, to do the work it would take to repair the irrigation channels to bring water to fields after lying fallow for two planting seasons? The cleaning and repair of their old homes? To bringing life back to the stone buildings?

There was also the retrieval of Iah. Chances were good he was still buried in the riverbed. It was not a long journey from Sharvik, but the trek, plus digging him up and transporting him would take more time. At least there would be more people to accomplish those tasks than when the idol was buried.

CHAPTER 10

Shapes flashed by in the surrounding darkness. It was impossible to tell who or what moved so quickly. It seemed to be everything and everyone along its own timeline, spaced so as not to collide with another moving body.

Colors, bright and muted, dark and light, everywhere. Growing as if living within themselves. Shrinking as if dying alone. Nothing depended on or joined with anything else. Somehow, that meant love did not exist. If true, then feelings, which controlled every individual, did not exist.

However, when Magan looked carefully, she found them. Hiding behind and within those things visible, waiting to be found, shadows giving impetus and force to all else existing in this world. At last, she found even love, for it must be there, alongside other emotions, but strongest of them all.

Images of power, death, defeat, longing flashed through the darkness. Her breathing was shallow, all energy concentrated, seeking, learning. If she were lying down and not sitting cross-legged on the temple floor, an observer might have thought her dead.

She felt it when Brynja gently closed her eyelids with her fingertips. For a day and a night, she was guided through deep meditation, knowing her teacher watched for signs of wrongness in the internal journey. When she cried out several times and whimpered in the middle of the night, Brynja's touch calmed her

Magan's eyes opened. Tears ran down her cheeks and she slumped with exhaustion. She didn't acknowledge the woman who helped her to a pallet. After drinking a great quantity of water, she slept for a full day. On waking, she recognized Brynja, watched her every expression, even though the blue-eyed gaze often made her want to look away. Those eyes were so piercing, strength and assuredness emanating from her inner self.

Magan licked the last crumbs of bread from her fingers and drank from the waterskin. She had no idea what should happen next and looked ahead with an atypical dread of the unknown.

"You stayed longer than most other students on their first guided meditation," Brynja said. "Meditating on your own helped, but you need structure, discipline. What did you see?"

Magan brought her gaze to the other woman's face, trying to see in the blue eyes what she wanted or expected to hear. So much appeared out of the darkness of her meditation. How to describe them, name them? Images flashed before her conscious vision, reappearing unbidden and well-remembered, overshadowing the blue eyes.

"There were colors," she said at last. "All of those of the rainbow and shades in between. There were some I could not quite see, yet I knew they were there. Objects were without substance, were formless, but possessed power."

Magan paused, remembering, a smile playing across her lips. It passed as she spoke again.

"The shapes were difficult to see, as if incomplete. Some of them were personality traits like meanness, morality, sense of humor, each having its opposite somewhere near. Within and around them, the emotions ..."

Brynja laughed.

Magan stopped, embarrassed. She was saying it so badly, unable to find the right words or combination of words to describe the actions, maybe purpose, of the emotions.

"I did not laugh at you. Go on."

Magan nodded, then continued. "I've meditated before. I've never gone so deeply within myself, never seen my own darkness, the depths of despair, selfishness, fear. Everything floating, glowing like small bubbles in sunlight. At first the emotions were without purpose. They just floated aimlessly.

"Then I saw they never touched one another, yet they were a part of everything. Each personality trait, each person I might be, was ... Those bubbles were the light in the darkness."

Again, she stopped unable to describe how something could be a part of, yet not touch, everything else. Each emotion maintained separateness, their own identities never melding with others.

"They were always separate and a part of all," Brynja said, as if encouraging her.

"Yes. They acted as the moving force and the barrier, which held them in check."

"It's difficult for us to conceive of something which is one thing and its opposite, dark and light, male and female," Brynja said. "That is why you have such difficulty describing it. You saw it. You understood it with your emotions. You could not understand it with your logic. Although always a part of our very lives, it is not a part we can readily see."

"Was it real? Or did I create it in my imagination?"

"Real or not, it existed for you. It is part of the oneness with the sword you will one day experience. The oneness with every-thing around you."

Magan smiled. They had been working together for more than three weeks, and although she accepted such learning would take time, she chafed at the seeming lack of progress.

"How much longer will it take to learn everything?"

Brynja laughed again. "A lifetime, my girl."

Magan blushed. She had never felt her youth so strongly before. The teacher, although older, appeared wiser and more self-assured than the age difference would account for. She phrased the question badly, and Brynja always answered exactly what she asked, not what she meant. "How long to learn everything you can teach me?"

"The same. I have a lifetime's experience behind me."

Magan wondered from the first moment she appeared how old Brynja might be. She looked ageless, yet decades of expe-rience shone behind those eyes. Where did she come from? Her pale skin and blue eyes were so different from anything or anyone in Magan's experience. When their arms or hands were next to each other, Magan looked at her own browner skin differently.

From the first moment, she was fascinated by the blue eyes. Brown and grey eyes were common among her people. Sometimes green like her own, but those were rare. Brynja's were the first blue eyes. The color was sometimes bright, like the sky on a clear, sunny day. When thinking intensely, they turned dark, again like the sky, but when the sun was nearly set. Other times, especially when she laughed, they sparkled like sunlight reflecting off the river. The one time she got angry, they turned darker, nearly purple.

At first, Magan was suspicious, remembering Friya's pose as Kira. Hers was a flawed impersonation Magan had seen through. Brynja, too, was wary at first, evident from her reluctance to share how she knew to come.

"You called me," was all she said at first. When Magan asked how she called and how she was heard, the response was a shrug and, "Later."

Each day started with a run through the empty streets of Sharvik. The sun was low, casting the streets into tunnels of shadow and cool air, yet she worked up a sweat. Afterward, a first meal and they talked as they ate. Brynja outlined the days ahead.

"We won't have as much time as I usually spend with a student."

"Why not?"

"Your people will soon be on their way back. Their journey will be hard and long, but I will be gone before their arrival."

"There's no reason you must leave then."

"You are well ahead of most students. You've fought for your life. You've encountered others with power and overcame them. You've explored the abilities you were born with and raised them to new heights within the limitations of having no formal training. When I leave, you will have learned most of what I can teach you."

Magan had learned the teacher knew much about her and wondered whether the woman could read her mind, look through her memories. She'd also described the highlights of the adventures she experienced in the past: the encounters with Friya, a struggle which stretched her own powers to the breaking point.

"I want to know everything. My—what would you call them—skills? talents? abilities? How much more can I learn? Is there a limit to what one can do?"

"There are always limits," Brynja said, a slight smile on her lips. "And a price to pay."

Magan started to ask again where the older woman came from but refrained. A suspicion was growing, though, the journey was through time and space, made possible by magic.

After the meal, they practiced with weapons. Magan loved working with the sword, but Brynja had brought many types of weapons with her, some totally unknown in the land. Spears were common, but she had never used one. What the teacher showed her was less heavy, limber, and more easily wielded. She particularly liked a blade longer than a knife, shorter than a sword, good for close-in fighting

Other weapons were laid out on the floor of her quarters, the purposes of which weren't clear until Brynja taught her. Along with the swords, both short and long and the wooden staff, a strange weapon of two short pieces of wood joined by chains and an ax, heavy and unwieldy. The names were odd. It was the longer sword Magan saw as a treasure. It was called a katana, made from the finest steel, a metal unknown in Magan's world. Her own sword was bronze and, according to Brynja, not nearly as strong.

"It comes from a distant land and time I visited many years ago. I've treasured it."

"Why should I learn these weapons when I will never use them in a real fight?" Magan was testing the weight of the wonderful sword, slashing the air, swinging it in circles from side to side, reveling in its balance.

"It's important to learn to adjust to many types of weapons. It helps to think differently, move differently, look at your opponent's weapons and determine how they are used. Be flexible, both in your thinking and actions."

"How did you come by so many different ones?"

"I travel."

Magan nodded, knowing the teacher would tell her in her own time, if at all. She also wanted to know how a person could move them from one place to another.

They prepared for the day's practice. On this day they moved outside of the gates of the village. Although the central square was large with the temple forming one boundary and public buildings the other three, outside was bigger, away from the walls, giving them room to expand their movements.

As she abandoned the katana and swung her own sword, Magan felt the freedom of being in an open space. She liked the absence of echoes. They worked their way back and forth, side to side, on the hard-packed earth, loosening up at first. Their strokes were choreographed to create muscle memory. If the opponent strikes from one side, you counter with the proper stroke. It was a routine of attack and defend, and they took turns.

They practiced in this way often enough the mind, although aware of what was happening, became disengaged. The body itself, all of the necessary muscles, moved in a rhythm. Step, swing, parry, high, low. The clang of blade against blade.

Magan raised her arms to swing the sword up, then down, expecting Brynja to raise her sword horizontally to block. Instead, she spun around, moving to Magan's side, forcing the tip of her sword down to the ground. Before she could turn to face her teacher, Brynja touched her side.

"You would be dead now."

"Yes."

"Never extend yourself fully. When you raised the sword all the way, you had nowhere else to go. You were flat-footed, also leaving yourself no way to move, to counter."

She demonstrated how Magan could have countered the move. They practiced each step and swing slowly, over and over.

When done, they agreed to hold practice sessions outside the gates in future. The open space gave them greater flexibility, room to move, and the sounds didn't echo around them.

CHAPTER 11

The days went by. One evening, Brynja and Magan set off for a walk after their last meal. Brynja explained the gift of magic while they walked through the quiet streets and alleys.

"When one has many years' practice of magic and meditation," she said quietly, "one can hear the unspoken voices of others."

Their footsteps echoed through the lane. Magan felt pleasantly engulfed in her surroundings and the sound of Brynja's voice, although in the back of her mind, she missed the sounds of villagers making Sharvik feel alive.

"Newly awakened magical spirits call out for help, for a teacher. Sometimes they don't even know it. Those are the voices teachers hear. They draw us to them, and we are almost compelled to answer. It is one of the things you may look forward to if you become skilled in what we call magic."

Her words penetrated the pleasant fog. She was telling what Magan had asked a dozen times.

"That's how you heard me?"

Brynja nodded.

"Is your home near Sharvik?" Magan asked.

"No. I come from very far away in both time and space."

"But you said you heard me only a few days before you arrived. To get here in so short a time, your home can't be too far." Magan shook her head. "Sometimes I don't understand you at all."

They had returned to her house and sat on the blankets spread on the floor. Magan stirred the coals in the firepit and put more wood on the fire. Flames reflected from the metal of the weapons lying close together on the floor to one side.

"Is it ever inconvenient?" she asked when she settled down.

"You mean, would I sometimes rather not answer the call?" Magan nodded.

"Often. A few times I have not."

"How did it make you feel?"

"A little sad at first, until I found out there is always someone else who answers the call. Quite often the first person to hear is the nearest but not the right one. After a time, it goes beyond the first person to another. It's as if we are all connected by what goes on in our minds and spirits."

"Did the others help you get here from so far away in only a few days?"

"No, but many can do as I did."

"Another time and place?" Magan murmured.

"Maybe you will experience it someday," she said. "You have the means now."

"What do I have that could lead me to your home?"

"May I see the medallion?"

She pointed at the medallion hanging from a black, braided cord around Magan's neck. It was the one she found in the courtyard the night Iah was stolen. She hid it in her house, planning to check it out when the village settled down. It was forgotten until she and Dzorin returned. She rarely wore it, knowing as she did others like it were worn by Friya and her warriors.

She pulled the cord over her head and handed it to Brynja, who held the medallion in the palm of her hand. In the firelight, the stones, which always looked black until touched, now glowed in several deep colors. One was red, another green, the third amber, and the fourth blue. Brynja turned the medallion, and the colors swirled. Then she held it closer, studying the stones. She touched them randomly ... and disappeared.

Magan scooted backwards and looked around the room. She got to her feet slowly and retreated until her back pressed against the wall. She stared at the place where Brynja had been seated. She swallowed hard and checked the whole room. As she turned her head, shadows flickered against the walls, seen from the corners of her eyes. Quickly, she turned again, thinking to catch sight of Brynja playing a game of hide and seek in the open. Even she could not move so fast.

Her next thought was to check outside, and she started toward the door.

"I'm here, Magan."

She whirled around to find Brynja sitting on the floor opposite from where she disappeared. Magan's hand flew to her mouth. "So, you are," she whispered. "How ..."

Brynja held the medallion out, and Magan took it, handling it tentatively now. She wound the cord around her hand and sat down. Holding it toward the fire, she again saw the colors dance within the stones and felt afraid. Looking up, she saw an identical medallion in Brynja's hand.

Magan held out her medallion. "Teach me."

"Not now."

"I need to know." Her voice was urgent, demanding, and Brynja looked at her with eyebrows raised.

"What bothers you?" she asked.

Although Brynja knew about Friya, Magan now filled in the details, at first hesitantly. The memories, so very painful, locked away, and unresolved, although she thought they were dealt with sufficiently. As she finished the story of the witch's seduction of Dzorin and supposed final demise, tears blurred her vision and she sniffed them away. Suddenly, she wished she had not told everything, did not want to remember. Dzorin's betrayal was too personal.

"You are right, Magan. This Friya probably is not dead, although you must have injured her greatly. Otherwise, she would have pursued you. Her sort will not give up. There are many different kinds of magic, none of them good or evil. Some people practice more kinds than others. The person's soul is either light or dark.

"There are those who believe there is a lord of darkness, a completely evil being, with no good to him—or her, depending on the belief system. However, you will find nothing totally good or totally evil in this world or your inner world. Every being is a combination of both, every thought has two sides, just as you saw when you meditated. Some tend more to one side or the other, but neither good nor evil is perfect. They are only represented by individual gods of our own making."

"Even Friya?"

Brynja nodded. "Even Friya. Corrupted by the power she possesses, even she is not wholly evil."

"Iah told me some of those things," Magan said after a time.

"Iah?"

"Yes," she said. "He is our primary god here in Sharvik, the very one carried away in the night and in whom I don't believe. In Mari and, I think, in Hattushah, he is a minor god, but my people believe in him, depend on him. After he was lost to us, everyone left, apparently convinced life could not continue here without his blessings.

"His loss was what led to our meeting Friya and our misadventures."

Brynja nodded. So many things happened over the past year in Magan's life and Brynja spoke of various events without having every detail. Even to Magan's ears, the god she didn't believe in speaking to her was one of the more bizarre.

However, memories of her time with Dzorin were achingly personal. Magan was so absorbed in the new learning, she hardly thought of him since Brynja arrived. Thinking of him now brought the ache for him, for the warmth of his body next to hers, the sound of his voice. However, it also brought memories of the bad moments. Those she would rather forget.

"It's late," Brynja said, seeming to sense her mood. "We should get some sleep. I do want to hear more details of your adventures in the morning."

Magan talked the next morning and every day thereafter, opening up to this teacher as never before with anyone else, even Dzorin. Brynja was older, and she shared the same kind of difference Magan always tried to hide. Did the teacher live in a society where she must hide her gifts, too? Were people of power admired, not condemned, where she came from? Did women openly follow any profession or work they wanted? No matter how she broached the subject of the teacher's background, answers were always vague and elusive.

Pleasing Brynja was very important. Other than missing

Dzorin—although not as often as she thought she should—performing well was the most important part of her life now.

Magan wondered if the new feelings inside her were born from a long-hidden need for her mother. Did she look at Brynja in the same way as well as seeing her as a teacher? Magan trusted her, was comfortable with her in a way new to her. Except for the aunt who raised her, the women of Sharvik always shunned her, although she tried hard to fit in for a long time. She eventually gave up and accepted she was neither like them nor one of them. As the years passed, it became less and less important.

For days, teacher and student practiced the martial arts. Additional physical training—running, strengthening—went well. It was her attempts to turn her focus inward again which proved difficult in spite of the earlier meditations. It was a means to strengthen her internal powers, to find the abilities she'd suppressed most of her life.

Brynja never lost patience with that part of the practice even after Magan failed to repeat the experience several times. Once, she came close, but was unable to describe what she saw any better than the first time.

"Understanding will come with each experience. Then the words will come easily," Brynja assured her.

The days were spent in the physical routines. At night, Magan recited over and over the spells, then tried different types of sensitive powers, strengthening those she did have and testing for others she might develop, using all of the senses, not just her eyes and touch.

When they began, her ability to move objects without touching them was the strongest. Until she'd turned the mercenary's sword, forcing him to cut his own throat, it was a power she'd used little. Oh, she'd used the ability to help lift the idol, but with the physical strength of Dzorin, Vanthi, and her own, it was easier. It was different with the warrior who fought against her. He was strong. And she did the deed in desperation, to save herself and her friends.

They explored other talents, too. At certain times, Magan often thought she heard others' thoughts. Brynja taught her to listen with her mind, with limited success so far. Projecting her own thoughts proved even more difficult.

"Does someone have to have the same ability to hear me?"

"It helps, although it is possible to make other people hear. Many, though, are totally deaf to such expressions."

"When I am better at it, will I be able to control what I hear?"

"You do it now without realizing it. Granted, this is a skill you don't use often. But your mind does it for you."

They tried to practice communicating with each other with their minds, but without much success. "We'll work on it," Brynja said.

"Magan, how well do you think you know yourself now?"

Magan stared into the fire, considering the question and chewing the last bite of bread of their evening meal. More than two months had passed since Brynja arrived, two days since being guided through the memories of finding Iah. She followed instructions implicitly, even when she thought what was asked was useless at best. Brynja knew her better than anyone on earth.

Magan came to know her, too, although not quite as well, since the blue-eyed woman revealed little of herself. They shared Brynja's food and ate boiled lentils and beans she and Dzorin found in sealed jars, slept near one another for warmth in the night; Brynja comforted her one night when bad dreams of Friya woke her, holding her until the tears stopped.

But as to this question ...

"I'm not sure," she answered truthfully. "At times, I think there is nothing about myself I don't know. Then something happens—a stray thought from nowhere, a feeling or memory I thought I had dealt with—and I am surprised."

"We never know everything, except, so my teacher told me, on the day we die. It all becomes clear then, and we wonder why we couldn't see it before." Brynja looked sober then grinned suddenly. "I always wondered how he knew when he was clearly still alive."

Magan laughed then grew quiet. Her thoughts turned to what kept her awake part of the night. With a little more than two months gone, Dzorin was probably on his way back, leading their people home. Brynja had said she would be gone before the villagers' return. Would Brynja be able to teach her everything, or enough, in the time left to them? Perhaps they would be finished by then. She didn't know how much more work she needed, how much more she could learn, but the thought of her teacher leaving brought such sadness.

Brynja broke into her thoughts.

"It's time to meld your new self-knowledge with your physical abilities."

"In what way?"

"You are adept with a sword."

Magan nodded. They practiced together repeatedly and her technique was much improved. She was stronger than ever, and her ability to anticipate increased.

"There is a way to join your mind with the weapon, make it a part of you and you a part of it. The weapon can become an extension of your powers, both physical and mental, wielded so naturally you won't have to think at all. Every motion becomes as quick as thought.

"For instance, when you parry a blow. You have to move the sword very quickly. Sometimes you can do it as if you knew how the blow would come as soon as your adversary did."

"It happens occasionally," Magan admitted. "I have noticed it more when I fought for my life rather than practice."

"And you react to an opening as if you expect it. Of course, you do this in the way you thrust, parry, and defend. But you can react to the openings even faster if you become one with your sword.

"It works not only with the sword, but with other weapons, too. You can become one with all life around you. You become it, and it becomes you. You become your enemy—"

"My enemy?" Magan interrupted. "If that's true, how could I kill him?"

"It's no longer a matter of killing when this happens. The weapon does not take a life."

The words did not make sense. Magan could see Brynja was trying to organize the thoughts in her mind so the words were right. She shook her head in frustration.

"Not all of my students have been warriors, but to the ones who are, it has been difficult to explain. It is something one can only experience, not describe. I can only tell you, with much practice in blending your physical actions with the meditation I have taught you, it can be done.

"One stage presents a red haze. Your vision, everything you see, is tinged with red. Later, sound stretches out, grows thin. In this stage, you are one with everything around you. The sword is you. Your adversary is you. The world is you. Some teachers refer to it as the void, the moment when nothing matters, yet everything matters."

"You have achieved these?"

"The red haze, yes, several times, and I have experienced the void, although only twice. I still practice with the hope someday I can enter the void easily. The day will come if I live long enough, I suppose." Brynja smiled. "Right now, it's time to practice."

Magan rose and gathered her weapons. However, her attention was divided. More than ever, she anticipated feelings of loss when Brynja would be gone.

CHAPTER 12

Once more, Magan meditated, delving into memories this time, relating the details to Brynja.

"I see a large body of men. Several of them are ghostly white, lighter skin than yours. Not like you, more as if they are painted white. Some are black-skinned.

"They are waiting. They are soldiers of some kind. Warriors. Raiders. They have three wagons."

She stops, looks closer. A shrouded figure sits atop one of the wagons.

"I know that wagon. And Iah under the cloth."

Brynja touched her shoulder lightly and her excitement calmed. "What is happening?" she asked softly.

"Three smaller groups of men are camped in the immediate area. All of their leaders are meeting. One of them raises the shroud, shows them the idol. Now, they look at the other wagons. They seem to be … Yes, they're haggling."

Magan was quiet for some time, watching the scene unfold. *She will be a part of it, yet still in the past. Now, she is an observer, seeing what happened before she and Dzorin caught up with the raiders.*

Each of the small groups takes a wagon or two to its camp. Four of the warriors go with Iah. Everyone looks satisfied with their bargain.

The three smaller groups take down tents and pack everything onto camels and wagons. In a short time, they all move off. Magan turns back to the larger party. Time moves faster. Another party of warriors arrives, as large as the first, the warriors mingling, merging into one army. She knows all of them were involved in the raid on Sharvik.

The leader stands on slightly higher ground, shouting orders. Every man holds a medallion. She watches as they touch the stones randomly and jumps in surprise as they all disappear.

"Follow them," Brynja whispers.

"How?"

"Don't ask. Do it!"

Magan reaches out like one feeling her way in the dark. She moves forward without knowing if she walks, runs, or flies. The figures of the warriors appear ahead, transparent, moving swiftly. They cannot see her, for she is not there. Or is she? Are the warriors there? They move forward through flashing lights brighter than stars, their breathing is easy.

They stop suddenly, their forms no longer transparent. They have substance. Their arms and legs move as they take their fingers away from the medallions and mill around on a smooth green carpet.

In the distance, Magan sees a tall building of dark stone. Round, pointed roofs jab at the sky around a larger one. Sunlight reflects off all of them, yet she senses the air is cool.

"Brynja. Where am I? How do I get back?"

"Simply turn and follow the trail." The voice sounds very far away, and she becomes more frightened. "Don't think. Feel. Imagine."

Magan takes a deep breath and turns. Behind her, a trail of sparks leads the way. She senses the little flashes of fire will not last very long and hurries. Back. Flying. Running. Still without a sense of movement. It grows dark.

She opened her eyes. Brynja sat near, staring into the fire. *She saw through my eyes.* She studied her teacher's profile and began to understand other things.

Two swords glinted in the sunlight. Metal striking metal, the sound echoing through the deserted square, even into the temple through the open door. Magan followed the sound inside, floated with it through cracks and niches in the walls. She and the sounds wrapped around a torch sconce.

The sword flew from her hand, banging against the wall of

the near building, crashing to the stones set deep in the ground.

"Magan! Concentrate!"

She looked up, her empty hands spread before her. Brynja held her own sword raised, pointing at her with anger for the second time.

"You could get killed."

"How did you—?"

Brynja strode to the sword and picked it up. Magan hadn't moved, confused by what happened.

"Where were you?" Brynja asked as she handed back the weapon.

"I was in the temple," she answered after a moment. "I followed the sound of our swords as it drifted inside. I floated into the little openings in the walls, over the rafters in the ceiling. I wrapped around one of the sconces in the wall. How?"

"It's the sort of thing I talked about, becoming one with your sword and everything around you. You were too focused on the sound, but it shows you can do it properly with more practice."

Magan, still confused and amazed, said nothing. The experience was both frightening and exciting. Brynja called a halt to practice for the day.

"It was as if I left my body," Magan said as they walked toward the temple. "I saw and did things I couldn't possibly have done. Like with the medallion." She stopped. "What if I wasn't able to come back?"

"You didn't leave your body either time. Your perceptions simply went beyond their normal limitations."

"Nothing could keep me from coming back to myself?"

"Oh, there are ways of becoming trapped, but your spirit and your mind are still with your body. It's like casting a net. A larger one covers more area."

"I'm not sure …" she started to say, then shook her head.

"The medallion allows your physical self to move from place to place, time to time. That is where you could become trapped. But you will learn another day."

For the next few days, they practiced often, but Magan would not try the melding of action and meditation. Brynja did not push, and she was grateful. In spite of what her teacher said,

Magan was unable to completely throw off the fear she would extend outward and be unable to return.

Magan felt apprehensive. They were practicing outside the village gates again. Brynja was clearly distracted, her tension transferring to her student. Was she contemplating leaving soon? Was she worrying on some level about Magan's progress?

"Wait!" the teacher called out. Her sword was only half raised.

Startled, Magan changed the trajectory of her blade just in time. "What is it?"

"Look." Brynja pointed toward the desert behind Magan. Five figures approached. They were nomads, men, possibly hunters or just as possibly, raiders. The two women were so engrossed in their practice the newcomers came close to them and the gates.

"We can get inside and close the gates," Magan said. When she looked toward the gates, however, their mock fight had placed them too far to reach them. The visitors splashed across the river, now at its low stage.

"We must be prepared to fight," Brynja said. She looked all around, making certain there was only one group

Magan nodded. She couldn't help welcoming the possibility of a real fight. Practice honed her skills. However, a fight with a real adversary was much more exciting. She was also eager to see her teacher in a real fight.

The man in the lead raised a hand in greeting. He smiled and moved his hands out to either side, showing they were empty. The four men behind him did not show their hands. They wore short beards in the nomad style. Their cloaks fell below knee-length and were shades of beige, nearly the same as the variations in the sand and dirt of the desert. Their tunics and trousers draped loosely, each man in a different color: red, green, blue, yellow, and brown. It was as if these outfits were intended to identify them separately.

Magan returned the greeting and waited for the man to speak. Ordinarily, she would have welcomed them, hoping for news or stories. These strangers were not contemplating any of those; they balanced on the balls of their feet, their thoughts strong enough for her to sense they were ready for action. She remained silent, expecting a fight.

"We would speak to your head man," the leader said.

"He isn't here at present," Magan said. Tension in each man filled her mind, slightly overwhelming

Concentrate, Magan. This is what we train for.

Brynja's words calmed Magan. She nodded slightly, acknowledging her teacher's instructions.

"Ah, he's away." The men behind him looked at each other and smiled. "Is there a second in charge?"

"We are in charge."

"You? The two of you?" His smile widened. "We saw you practicing with your swords. Are you Amazons or such?" He looked around at the other men, one of them laughed. "Are there any men within the walls of your village we can speak with?"

"What is it you need?" Magan kept her gaze on the leader. She held the sword with the handle in one hand and the blade lying across the palm of the other. Brynja held a similar bronze sword she used when they practiced rather than the steel blade, but the katana lay on a cloth nearby, with other weapons.

"We saw the two of you practicing with the swords as we approached," the man repeated. "You looked as if you are experienced with the weapons."

"The water in the river is clean," Magan said. "We've no food to spare right now."

"Your swords look well-made. May I see that one?" He took a step closer to Brynja and pointed at the katana lying between her and Magan and slightly behind. "I've never seen its like before." His companions spread out behind him, forming a half-circle.

"No."

"I insist."

"No."

Brynja took two steps closer to Magan and adjusted her sword to a ready position. Magan kept her eyes on the leader. He undid his cloak and flung it aside. The others followed suit. Each wore a common sword in a scabbard in his belt.

"We don't want to kill you," he said. "We just want your weapons."

The men spread farther on either side, intending to encircle the two women. Brynja turned slightly sideways to face the two on her side. She looked relaxed, yet ready. Magan felt herself grin. These men were about to learn a valuable lesson, and she looked forward to teaching them. There was no doubt in her mind she and Brynja could give these men the fight of their lives.

The men hesitated. Perhaps they had never fought against women before. Or they might fear men would come rushing through the open gates and attack them. Still, there was an arrogance in the way they looked at her and Brynja which irritated her. Time passed and still they hesitated. No men appeared. They seemed certain the skills of the two women were less than their own, and they kept one eye on the opening into the village.

The man in the green tunic to Magan's right took a step toward her. She stood straighter and raised her sword. The leader must have given a sign, one she couldn't see, and green tunic attacked. At the same time, the man in the brown tunic attacked Brynja. The two women took the first blows, sword against sword, with ease. Magan's blood was up, and instead of waiting for him to back off and renew the attack, she moved forward, swinging with precision and power.

CHAPTER 13

Dzorin spotted Sher running to catch up as the last of the wagons rolled through the narrow gap between two hills. The long caravan was four days out from Hattushah, their progress slow since everyone except the weakest walked.

Dzorin studied the faces of the people moving past him. It was early morning and they were already tired. He could see it in the way they walked, the expressions on their faces. But they moved forward, their eyes focused on the road leading them on. They were going home. Julin worked miracles, pushing and cajoling until willingness to begin the journey became strong in most. Their home was Sharvik, and when Iah returned, their village and their lives, would be good again.

Since the council of elders who had made civic decisions in Sharvik fell apart when they left the village behind, a new council was formed just before departing Hattushah. Some of the same elders were included and younger members were added. They still needed to learn to work together before they were strong enough as a group to override Garaf and his priests.

Garaf was considered to be Amleth's choice to succeed him, although in the absence of Iah, no one could be named high priest. With the breakdown of the council, he had made most of the decisions while they lived in Hattushah, taking his cue from priests in the city, who only answered to the king, and Crosus, their landlord. Seeing themselves as the leaders, the priests gave up control with bad grace. Garaf looked askance at Dzorin whenever Dzorin looked his way, and particularly angrily at Julin, who he felt was betraying them

Even as he resented the priesthood's losing control, Garaf

considered it was only proper for their wagons to be in the fore-front, thus avoiding dust and any following danger. Dzorin put them in the lead to better keep an eye on them, so they were both satisfied with the arrangement.

Unlike his colleagues, Julin shared Dzorin's desire to get their people home. They pushed everyone into returning to Sharvik, in the process becoming the leaders of the journey since the priests wanted nothing to do with it and the elders were more of a loose gathering than a working committee. Varas, captain of the guard, was a military man with no taste for governing, so he declined leadership. He contributed to the planning on every level but would not make any decisions.

The priests, although loath to give up any authority, did not want to be blamed when it all went wrong and also left plan-ning to them. Two of their numbers remained in Hattushah just in case it all failed and to keep Garaf's name in the minds of those in power. They would see the people were welcomed back to the capital with open arms.

For four days, the trek went well. The people were in good spirits and, although progress was slow, they were getting their wind, becoming stronger, in spite of appearances. The lapsed time was long enough to make Dzorin wonder if Crosus had given up on keeping them on the barren land.

The caravan was out of sight while Dzorin and the others watched Sher loped near. He and the other warriors could now run all day, putting leagues behind them. When he drew closer, It was possible to see his jaws were tight, the muscles working under the skin. His hands held tightly to the spear he carried. He'd spotted a threat.

From the first day, Dzorin placed warriors behind and ahead, and some of the farmers to either side of the caravan, instructing them to watch for any signs of trouble. If they saw anything, they were to bring word to him. But he expected any real threat would come from behind. It appeared he was right.

His fears rose from a general need for caution, although how Crosus would react to their leaving gave him reason to worry. The possibility was their landlord might follow or actu-ally send his personal troops to bring them back. He had sent word through his collector and Garaf they could not leave until he released them, even as the people of Sharvik packed up their belongings. Dzorin suspected it was the priests who kept the landlord informed of their plans, and after his adventures of the past year, he trusted few people and expected the worst. For that reason, he held off telling the priests the exact time for departure until two hours before, barely giving them enough time to pack up, but not enough time to contact Crosus.

"We must notify Lord Crosus," Garaf protested. He'd tried to send one of his priests into Hattushah to notify them.

"Best not to," Dzorin said. He'd left two warriors to oversee the priests' final packing, ordering them to not let any of them out of their sight. Crosus would know soon enough.

Sher stopped in front of Dzorin. Earlier in the day, Dzorin had noticed a thin veil of dust rising in the distance behind them. He watched it continue to rise while his fellow warrior bent over with hands on knees to catch his breath.

"You're out of shape, Sher," Dzorin said with a little laugh.

The warrior grinned. "A little." Sher straightened. "We're being followed. Twenty, thirty men. Two each in three chariots. The rest on foot." He sounded excited as if looking forward to a fight.

"Did you see them closely enough to recognize them?"

"They carry Crosus's standard."

"I guess paying an extra month's rent wasn't enough," Dzorin said. He never expected it to work, but it was worth a try.

He surveyed their surroundings. Varas approached from the hills as the caravan pulled ahead. The captain had moved ahead with the people to ensure they made it through the pass safely. The other warriors now hung back, recognizing the return of Sher must mean something, watching the serious conversation until Dzorin motioned for them to join in. Quickly, he explained the situation.

"Crosus probably didn't send a larger force because he never saw any of us as warriors," he said. "All he saw was a beaten group of refugees. We number seventeen, and with our swords there are no better soldiers. Varas taught us well."

Varas put a hand on his shoulder. "Others among us know how to fight," he said. "We won't be alone."

The warriors stood straight and proud. If they knew how pathetic they actually looked in their dirty, torn clothes and dull scabbards, it didn't show. Neither Dzorin nor Varas was going to tell them.

"Let the caravan move ahead. Three of you will stay close behind them in case Crosus's men get past."

He studied the landscape, strewn with boulders. Behind them, the land was flat with little cover. Ahead, their route rose between the two hills forming a narrow passage. Beyond, more hills, the path wider between them. If the caravan kept straight through the hills and Crosus's soldiers were intent on following them, it could prove to be an ideal trap. However, everything remaining equal, the wagons and people would not be far enough out of range to be safe. They would have to prevent the attackers from getting through the gap. The approaching warriors were likely trained and conditioned to run, with the chariots setting the pace, and they should catch up just after midday.

"They'll be quickening their pace," Dzorin said, nodding toward the pillar of dust. "They know we're within reach and will want to attack today." He turned and studied the pass again.

"We'll wait this side of the pass. Bowmen on the hills on each side. Dzorin pointed ahead to the passage through which the last of the caravan was just disappearing, at the same time looking at Varas for his approval. Their captain nodded.

"Are there any more spears? Swords? Knives, even?"

"A few," Varas answered.

"Dered, get them. See that those who are willing are armed in case Crosus's men get by us. Those men who guarded the flanks, probably. Bech, Cail, and Leod, go with him and provide a rear guard. Keep a close watch in all directions.

"Hein, you climb the hill on the right. Isik, up the left hill. Take the bows and as many arrows as you can carry. The rest of us, spread across the passage." There weren't many arrows since they'd concentrated on other needs for the journey, and he hadn't even thought of them during preparations. He figured no one else had either.

Looking back the way they'd come, he saw the rising dust draw closer. "They will catch up soon." He looked around them again and nodded. "This is the best place for a stand."

Everyone moved per his orders. For only a moment, Dzorin doubted whether he was doing everything necessary. He stepped into the role of leader because no one else did and began giving orders soon after he was reunited with them. Before, he was content to be the soldier, taking orders, never thinking about how things should be done, always leaving the decisions to others. He was exhilarated by this new role and surprised, too, when no one challenged him.

They waited and watched until the dust cloud widened, and the three leading chariots came into view. The horses stopped when near enough for the captain to be heard; the foot soldiers behind them slowed to a walk, forming ranks. Dzorin paced, studying the terrain, reviewing his options, and now moved to stand in the center of his line of warriors. Their numbers felt small compared to the new arrivals.

The pursuers continued toward them. Their footsteps could be heard and dust rose around them. The foot soldiers spread out behind the chariots, standing in three staggered lines. Pennants hung limply from the standards on both sides of the lead chariot. Sword scabbards and helmets reflected the brilliant sunlight. Crosus armed his little army well.

Dzorin took two steps forward. He and the officer in the lead chariot considered one another while the driver held a tight rein on the horses as they tossed their heads. They seemed as eager for a fight as the soldiers, in spite of the long trek.

"Why do you follow us?" Dzorin broke the silence.

"Lord Crosus wanted to know why all of you left his land without his permission," the captain said in an ingratiating tone. "He sent us to find you as soon as your absence was discovered. He feared you might be in trouble." He stood beside the driver who worked to control the horses as they pranced and jostled the chariot.

Dzorin nodded. "We told his collector we were leaving. Twice. We sent him word. We paid rent for three quarters plus one month. We are returning to our own village to rebuild our lives there."

"Lord Crosus is not pleased. Because of your lack of manners, he thinks you should return and apologize in person. To further make it up, you must also agree to stay on the land he leased to you another full year, until *he* decides it is time for you to leave."

"We are a free people who come and go as we will. The land was unhealthful and sterile. Nothing would grow there, and my people were becoming ill."

The land being unfit for habitation was probably one reason Crosus wanted them back. It would not earn him anything otherwise. Did these soldiers know they might also be about to engage in battle because their employer craved a woman in the caravan? Did the priests left behind urge him to take action? He suspected Garaf's priests had as much to do with this as anyone.

"It won't do." The captain said and drew his sword.

His driver tightened his hold on the reins of the nervous team. The trappings jingled. Some of the foot soldiers nocked arrows in their bows. A shout from the top of the rocks to Dzorin's right startled everyone. An arrow pierced the air, burying itself in the side of the captain's driver. The horses flung themselves against the relaxed tension on the reins. The captain grabbed for the reins, sword still in hand.

Dzorin jumped aside as the horses lunged forward. "Now!" he shouted. Under his breath, he cursed Hein for acting too soon.

His men behind him ran forward as arrows flew from the two warriors in the hills into Crosus's warriors. The foot soldiers from either side of the chariots loosed their arrows, but the warriors of Sharvik rushed forward and the arrows went into the ground. In the general confusion, the foot soldiers dropped the bows and reached for knives and short swords. Two were struck down by spears before they could pull their blades free of the scabbards. The others drew weapons, meeting the smaller oncoming force.

With a shout, Dzorin charged the lead chariot. The horses reared, still fighting the captain's control. Both animals appeared to be new to battle. However, the captain was not. Unable to calm the horses, he jumped from the chariot to meet Dzorin, abandoning what would have been a superior position if the horses were under control. Sharvik's men parted, letting the chariot and frightened horses race through their line.

All around him, Dzorin heard the clang of swords and the grunts of men as the two forces came together. He smiled at his adversary.

"One of us will die here, I think," Dzorin said.

The officer's eyes widened slightly, and Dzorin knew he made his point. It was always good to let the other know you don't care if the death is yours, even if you do. With the experiences of the past months, though, Dzorin often found he really did not care once a fight began.

The captain swung his sword in a high arc. Dzorin caught the blade against his own, pushed it to the side, bringing both blades downward. With the captain off-balance, he brought his own blade straight up from the ground, and the man jumped back barely in time. The captain's sword was still down, and Dzorin continued the swing of his own sword, bringing it right, then back across. It hit the other weapon, raised hastily. The man stumbled backward. Dzorin pressed the attack, swinging quickly in small, staccato strikes. The captain appeared surprised by Dzorin's skill.

Dzorin's heel landed sideways on a stone, twisting his foot slightly. To regain his balance, he turned, his back now to the horses of ananother chariot. They snorted and stamped their feet, distracting him. Given the opening, the captain struck, his strength compensated for his lack of quickness as he drove Dzorin backwards. The stomping horses sounded closer.

His adversary's gaze shifted between Dzorin, his sword, and the horses, judging his options. He swung harder, and Dzorin knew the horses' hooves were dangerously near. They gave him no room, neither right nor left. The only possible route was forward, over or around the captain.

Dzorin stood his ground against the next few strikes. He caught the sword against his own, taking the full impact with his body instead of giving with it. The captain swung wider, trying to put more weight behind the blow. Dzorin ducked under, rammed his left shoulder into the man's abdomen. He stumbled backward. Dzorin heard the sword point hit the ground behind him. He straightened, stepped around. With a shout he swung, caught the man in the side, and ripped upwards. A flood of pain darkened the man's eyes, and he slumped to his knees.

A scream rent the air and Dzorin looked around at the fight. It was winding down. Men from both sides lay on the ground, one of his own with an arrow protruding from his shoulder. Others held bleeding sword wounds. An enemy warrior lay absolutely still, either dead or dying. Two others of the injured were his own men.

Slightly behind him, in the direction of their trek, one of Crosus's men held onto a struggling woman. She kicked and screamed, her long hair writhing around her head, covering her face. Dzorin recognized Ileana nonetheless and ran toward her and her attacker.

"Stop, or I'll slice her throat!" the warrior called out.

It took only a moment to see he could do no such thing. The woman's struggles kept him from wielding his sword with any control. Dzorin walked toward the two. "Dzorin, help me," Ileana yelled.

"Let her go," he said when he stopped near them. "Or take her with you. Whichever you wish."

The warrior nearly dropped his prize. Ileana stared through strands of hair with a look of hurt and surprise.

"You can't …" the warrior began.

"Dzorin! What are you saying?" Ileana shouted.

"The fight is over," Dzorin said. "Your captain is dead."

The man looked around and released the young woman. She stood stock still, stunned by Dzorin's words. After a glance around, the warrior raised both hands, sheathed his sword, and walked past him toward his own comrades.

The battle lost momentum as Crosus's troop realized their leader had fallen. Swords were thrust and swung with less force. It was clear few of the men on either side had fought in some time. Practice was good, but actual battle made different demands.

"It's over," Dzorin shouted. Out of the corner of his eye, he saw Ileana walk away, toward the caravan beyond the rocks.

Everyone glanced his way with startled expressions. The scene of men standing frozen in awkward poses would have been funny had they not looked so serious, some with blood streaking the dust on their faces.

"It's over," he said again. He waved toward the captain, lying still, his blood mixing with the dirt around him. "Your captain is dead. Go home."

An under-officer stepped toward him.

"We can't return without you and your people. Crosus will have our heads."

Dzorin thought for a moment. "Tell him we outnumbered you. That more men joined us."

The lieutenant looked around at his men. They could go on fighting. More would die on both sides. He shrugged, apparently realizing the situation wasn't what they had expected. "I guess he couldn't argue with that," he said without conviction. His reluctance probably was more to do with unwillingness to accept responsibility for their defeat.

Their most seriously wounded men and the dead captain were loaded onto the chariots. All the bows and arrows were gathered up by Dzorin's men. They collected the swords and a few knives and placed them on the chariots among the wounded. The remaining officer watched while this was done, finally turning toward his chariot. He sheathed his sword automatically, as if he had forgotten it was in his hand. With bowed head, he climbed up, and from the look on his face, Dzorin guessed there would be more practice for these men if they survived Crosus's anger. Someone else would be made captain, at least.

Crosus's troop moved back the way they had come, shoulders slumped, feet dragging. The villagers won only because of practice and the discipline Varas drilled into them. However, one glance at the captain said Varas's men would be on the practice field as soon as possible. But they must reach Sharvik first. For the moment, there were wounds to bind and leagues to cover. The wonder of it all was not one warrior of Sharvik was killed. The wounded were helped to catch up with the caravan.

In spite of the officer's agreement to return to Hattushah, Dzorin left two men in the rocks to ensure the enemy kept moving away in the opposite direction.

CHAPTER 14

Brown water rushed headlong toward the sea. The river was at flood stage. Dzorin stood on the bank, mesmerized by the rush of water and the way sunlight glinted off the surface. He had seen the sea once and knew the rivers flowed to the sea. For a moment, he wished it would take him, too. After more than a year of roaming the known world, first with Magan and now with his people, he wondered if he would ever settle down to routine life in Sharvik. A part of him hoped he never again traveled so far from home, yet a part of him yearned to be like the river, always on the move.

He shook his head, chasing away the restlessness. He was on a long journey, for gods' sake, and he was tired. Right now, he was supposed to be deciding how to move his people across this river.

The flow was too strong and deeper than could be easily crossed on foot. The wagons could be lost, as heavy as they were. Flood waters were known to move boulders.

As if that wasn't enough, he worried about the mood of the people. With another barrier on their road home, many of them mumbled about turning back. Since they started out, several obstacles appeared to make their journey more difficult: Crosus's troop intercepted them. One of the wagons broke a wheel and had to be repaired. Garaf refused to travel on some sort of holy day no one else ever heard of. An unusual rainstorm, turning the road to mud, stopped them for a day.

Now, the flooding was early. What would this mean for planting new crops in Sharvik? The waters were needed for irrigation of the fields, for crops not yet planted. When he left the village, the irrigation channels and equipment were damaged. Was the Diyala in flood, too? If so, the flooding couldn't be doing the equipment any good.

Before leaving Hattushah, they had purchased as much food as they could: dried meats and fruits; lentils and grains, only one barrel of which was empty; two large jars of honey, which never went bad. Rations were divided up according to the number of days they expected to take for their journey. If it took many days longer—

"Can this be traversed?"

Dzorin turned to find Julin behind him, looking at the water as intently as he was.

"I don't know of a way to get across," Dzorin said.

"Can we wait until the river goes down?"

"It could take days. This river is wider than our Diyala. How long it stays at flood stage is anyone's guess."

They stood watching the surging waters in silence. Dzorin was coming up with and discarding ideas. When he had crossed the river on the outward journey, he was farther upriver, nearly three months ago. The width of the river then was no more than a quarter of what lay before him now. Lahnlee's camel waded through water no higher than its knees, crossing easily in two trips, first with the burden of goods and supplies, second with Lahnlee sitting on the animal, its long legs keeping its body and its burden high enough to stay dry.

"Some of the people are worried another attack may be coming up behind us," Julin said. "Sitting here as we are, we could be trapped."

"With the chariots and having no women or children, no doubt they would be faster than us. But they don't know, back in Hattushah, we're trapped here."

"No," Julin said. He picked up a stone and threw it toward the far riverbank. "But they do know they are faster and more maneuverable. Crosus might get the king to add his soldiers to those in his own employ. Money he is losing angers him. No one else would want to live on that land. Then there's Ileana."

And your fellow priests left behind? Dzorin wanted to ask. The young woman was becoming his own cross to bear. She appeared at the campfire several evenings, staying at a distance although watching his every move. His fellow warriors teased him about her having designs on him. He'd expected her desire for him to have abated after what he said during the skirmish with Crosus's troop. He tried others way to discourage her without hurting her feelings, but she wouldn't take the hint. Shaking his head, he brought his attention back to the moment.

"Could you say something to Ileana? Help her understand I can't return her affections?"

Julin shook his head. "I will try. But she won't believe me. Only you will she believe. I think she will end up hating you, no matter how gently you tell her."

Dzorin had told him what happened during the encounter with Cronus's soldiers, including his words to the soldier who held Ileana. Any words would be gentler than those.

"If the king becomes involved, things could be worse," he said changing the subject. "He and Crosus are related, after all, and he might support his kin."

He looked back at the camp. The people looked even more ragtag than before, using every bit of their possessions they could to create shelter for the moment. "If we manage to make it to Sharvik, will the king be angry with us? He could take away all protections or send an army to destroy our village. I'm not sure which would be worse."

The priest nodded. "We will have to petition the king after we get home. If we get home."

"The people—"

"I will do my best to keep them calm. There are enough who yearn for Sharvik to prevent the discontented from rebelling. How long, I cannot say."

Later, Dzorin met with Varas and others as he tried to work out a way to cross the river. The meeting was breaking up when Ileana came up to him. "I want to learn to be a warrior," she said in a low voice so only he heard.

He stared at her a long moment. Did this make the problem worse or better?

"Why. There are no other women warriors in Sharvik."

Before he could add, except Magan, she said, "Magan is a woman and a warrior. I want to be like her."

"You don't know her."

"I know she's a warrior."

He sensed there was something behind her request the young woman wasn't saying. Did she think by becoming a warrior she would be more attractive to him?

"I watched the fight at the pass," she said, looking away from him. "That man ..." She took a deep breath. "He grabbed me, and I couldn't defend myself. I want to be able to fight back."

Dzorin nodded. It was a better reason than he was imagining.

"Speak with Varas. He decides who trains as a warrior."

"Will you speak to him on my behalf?"

"I will speak with him once we get home."

She nodded and turned on her heel. It was much too soon to tell if this was a good thing, or not. The young woman was small but, given the way she struggled against Cronus's soldier, she might be stronger than she looked.

Sher grinned at Dzorin from across the fire. "What now," his friend asked.

He told his friend what Ileana asked. Sher chuckled. They sat in companionable silence.

Dzorin stared into the fire. He was so very weary, as were most of the people. So far, the trek had been exhausting. Three months passed, and the distance from the capital was not as many leagues as it should be. One good thing, though, was the delay caused by the swollen river could give time for people to regain some strength. True, living conditions weren't the best, but taking advantage of the situation was all they could do. At least Dzorin didn't have to spend much thought in keeping out of Ileana's way. For whatever reason, she stayed out of sight after she made her request.

At sunrise, Dzorin sent two warriors, one upriver and one down river, to check on any possible crossing. There might be a village or possibly a trade route where a bridge was built. Even a floating bridge would be good. He had heard of such a thing, although he'd never seen one. He had seen few bridges at all, come to that. It was possible they might find a ferry of some sort, something he'd also only heard of.

However, when Cail and Hein returned, neither discovered a bridge or a ferry. Cail thought there might be a good point at which they could cross safely down river. He had waded out then swam a few feet before being unable to find the bottom with his feet.

Hein still resented the dressing down Dzorin gave him after the fight with Crosus's troops. By sending him out to be alone with his own thoughts, it was hoped he would come to grips with his mistake. Apparently, it hadn't helped, as his report was given reluctantly and with attitude. He'd always been a bit of a rebel, and having the people depend on him hadn't improved his overall outlook. The gist of his report was there was no place affording an easy crossing.

The next day, the river was down, more so on the following day. It appeared flood stage was ending. If they could cross in another day or two, and at the rate at which they were traveling, they should be in Sharvik in a month. The food was holding out, and all of the vessels for water were kept filled in preparation for the day when they resumed their journey.

He and Julin stood again on the bank of the river two days later, surveying the situation. The eastern horizon glowed with the impending sunrise. The river was down a great deal during the night and was less than half the width blocking them the day before.

"We must keep an eye out for quicksand," Julin said. "One of us, maybe two, should walk ahead to check the river bottom."

"What's quicksand?" Dzorin asked.

Julin explained it was a mixture of sand and water which could suck a body under, never to be found again. The oxen and horses might be too big to disappear, but they could get bogged down, unable to move forward or backward.

"How do we check for it?"

"Probing with long poles."

"Why have I never seen it in our own river?"

"It has occurred there, although not in years." Julin closed his eyes, trying to remember. "I can't remember the last time I saw it. It may have been when there was an earthquake when I was a boy."

Dzorin wasn't certain he believed it existed. He'd crossed many rivers in the past months and lived alongside the Diyala his whole life. But he would not take any chances. He assigned three men to find long poles and Julin explained what they were looking for while he demonstrated how to probe the river bottom with a pole. Before the caravan started out, they checked a wide area from bank to bank. No quicksand was found, and they made ready to move across, in stages, a wagon at a time, along with the people to whom it belonged.

Instead of leading, the priests held back until three others proved it was safe. Their larger wagon carried the paraphernalia of their profession—golden artifacts, oil lamps, rugs—and Garaf, along with his two strongest supporters. Dzorin and Julin tried to get them to unload before crossing, lightening the wagon. There were enough priests to carry the items in small loads.

"Too much possibility something will be lost," Garaf argued.

He would not be convinced otherwise, insisting they cross as they were.

"Then the three of you could wade across," Dzorin suggested.

Garaf didn't bother to respond. He and his two minions kept their places in the wagon. The oxen were led slowly over the bank and into the water by another priest.

As they crossed the halfway point, they came to a sudden stop.

"What's wrong?" Dzorin shouted across.

"We are stuck!"

The priests kept tugging on the oxen, trying to make them pull harder, but the animals seemed to know their predicament better than did the men. Dzorin saw the wheels were bogged down and not the animals. The waters pushed against the upriver side, threatening to topple the wagon. Garaf, holding on tightly, shouting for Dzorin to do something after one of his minions fell into the water.

He sent every available man to the wagon to unload it. By lightening it and confirming the animals were not trapped, it should be possible to get it across. The remaining priest finally clambered down, but Garaf still refused to walk or help in any way, instead gripping the sides of the wagon until his knuckles turned white.

"Push, you dullards," he shouted.

With the weight lessened, and most of the priests ferrying items to dry ground, it appeared the wagon might turn in the current and drag the oxen with it. Some of the men stopped moving items from the wagon and strained to hold it steady. With all hands on the wagon again, the rig finally made its slow way into the shallows and up the slanted riverbank. The oxen were halted several feet from the water and stood with their heads hanging low.

Once safely on dry land, with Garaf sitting in it visibly and stiffly, they left re-loading it to the priests. They'd wasted enough time on this. But the lesson was learned: a wagon could be too heavy as well as too light.

No other wagon gave so much trouble, but there were different problems. One wagon got turned into the current and was barely caught before floating away. A hand cart was almost too low and nearly swamped. Again, several men worked to prevent disaster, lifting the cart and carrying it to the other bank. As for the rest, crossing slowly and carefully, one wagon at a time, lasted until the sun was setting. The goats and cattle were herded across as the sky grew darker. They made camp within sight of the river, relief at being on the opposite side giving them comfort.

For eleven days, they traveled faster and easier. The road was clear, and the weather held. Storms in the distance were visible, but only one caught them. The rain was gentle, although thunder and lightning made some uneasy. With spring upon them, everyone enjoyed the cool air of the early mornings.

After another early morning start, the sky to the east darkened. Dzorin, Varas, and Julin stood together, pondering the oncoming storm.

"Sandstorm," Varas said. The others nodded. "A big one."

"Strange, with all the rain that's been falling," Dzorin said.

"It's the desert," Julin said.

They needed to find shelter, but there was none.

"Form the wagons in a tight circle," Dzorin said. "Everything else in the center, especially the animals. Tie down everything. We'll have to make shelters for everyone."

He thought back to the sandstorm he and Lahnlee endured in the latter's tent. It was a strong, well-made, well-anchored shelter. They had nothing so good now.

As people worked to batten everything down, Garaf moved to the center of their circle. "Listen to me," he shouted, his voice rising above the quickening wind. "The gods—Iah—do not sanction our return to Sharvik. When the storm passes, we must return to Hattushah where we were safe. This journey is folly, dangerous. Even the wind and rain are against us."

His words were lost as the wind picked up. Only a few stopped to listen, anyway. Most worked frantically to protect themselves from the whirling sand. Soon, the sand would fill the air. Breathing would become nearly impossible. One's skin could be scrubbed raw.

Dzorin was too busy helping as many as he could to listen to or rebut the priest. He was beginning to believe it might be true the gods didn't want them to get home.

CHAPTER 15

The man in green backed up, surprised at Magan's attack. She continued pressing forward, forcing him to defend. Behind, she heard sword strikes and a sharp exclamation.

"My sword!"

She turned slightly to see the other men out of the corner of her eye. The one in orange crouched and came nearer, watching, looking for a good opening.

She struck at Green rapidly, not putting much power behind the strokes, but keeping him moving backward. Orange crept closer and she backed away from her first adversary, turned toward the newcomer, and all three froze, waiting for someone to make the next move. Magan wanted to glance over to see how Brynja was doing but didn't dare. Taking her attention from these two would give them an advantage.

She smiled, waiting for one of them to attack. It was Orange who darted forward, swinging his sword horizontally. When he swung it back, he was close enough for her blade to block his. She circled her blade, nearly twisting his sword from his hand. He stepped back to recoup.

Green appeared from the side and she swung toward him. He managed to block her blade, but he was surprised by how quickly her defense turned to offense. He, too, stepped back, rethinking his strategy.

Magan kept moving, not letting either man get behind her. She lunged at Green, then whirled to strike downward at Orange. Both attacks made them move toward each other. Behind her, sword striking sword rang out in rapid succession. Another exclamation. What was Brynja doing?

She lunged at Green, slipped past his defense, and the point of her weapon pierced his side. He gasped and stumbled back several paces. She turned again, facing Orange, who lunged at her, hoping to find her off guard. She barely raised her own sword in time to meet his blade. As he swung to her right, she jumped left and caught him in the shoulder with a downward stroke.

She continued moving around him. As she did, she had a chance to look over at Brynja. She'd believed her teacher was fighting against three of the nomads, but there were only two. Their leader kept himself distant, expecting his men to handle two women. His expression was puzzled at the very least, changing to disbelief.

The man in blue cried out in pain as Brynja caught his leg, slicing into his thigh. He went down as Magan turned back to her own struggle.

Both men's swords were down, Green nursed his side and Orange his shoulder. Neither man looked happy.

Magan twisted her sword in a circle at her side, waiting. With a thunderous look on his face, Green attacked, striking rapidly, one downward blow after another. She countered over and over, backing up. Tired of going backward, she slipped under his raised blade, moved behind him, and cut his sword arm. He dropped his sword as blood dripped to the sand. She stepped closer, lifted his sword with the tip of her own, and took it in her left hand.

Orange stood quite still, holding his free hand against the wound in his shoulder. He saw her disarm his companion, and frustration tightened his jaws. Suddenly, arms wrapped around her, pinning her own arms to her sides. The grip was tight, and she couldn't break it. The tip of her sword touched the ground. She tried to swing it enough to catch the man's feet or ankles but couldn't get enough movement.

Green, breathing hard, came nearer, one hand on his side, the other lifting the tip of his sword. He grinned as she stood perfectly still.

"We will teach you what a woman is good for," the leader said in her ear.

She expanded her chest and pushed with her arms against his. Letting out a deep breath, she dropped straight down, out of his grip, and rolled away. The leader shouted. Green rushed toward her. From the ground, she raised the tip of her sword as he came near and pierced his thigh. He bent over and grabbed his leg. Magan stood and kicked him on the other leg and he went down. The leader stepped clear.

One of Brynja's adversaries yelped in pain. The leader shouted words she couldn't understand. Orange and Green moved toward him, all three moving away from Magan. She turned and saw Brynja's opponents do the same.

The men grabbed up their cloaks and retreated. Two limped badly. One held his upper arm, blood oozing from his fingertips. Standing in a line again, they looked at the two women with less arrogance. This fight might be one they would never live down.

Magan walked over to Brynja, and the two of them watched as the men crossed the river and disappeared. A broken sword lay in the sand.

Magan realized the water was rising. Spring floods had begun early.

She moved to the bank of the Diyala, watching the brown water rushing past. The river was neither deep nor wide compared to the rivers she'd heard tales of. However, it was the lifeblood of the village, except now, the people weren't here to take advantage. The water ran past the fields, past the irrigation ditches. By herself there wasn't much she could do.

They should be here. How much longer before they returned? Before Dzorin returned? Could the planting season be saved?

For two days, the howling wind mimicked the voices of the villagers echoing around the lanes and alleys. They rushed past the doorway, moaning and crying. Magan grew restless and chafed at being confined to her house. The dust storm howled around and through the village, making conversation nearly impossible. Dust settled on everything, sifting through gaps in covered windows and doors into the rooms of her quarters and the temple.

For a week, the Diyala ran full and swift. Only days later it seemed, the winds picked up. The dust storm moved in and filled the air with sand and dirt for a full day and night.

Magan tried to concentrate on the sword and Brynja's instructions. After the nomads left, they resumed her training, building on the experience of the real fight. She used several weapons she never knew existed before. The staff had a long reach. The nunchaku were dangerous, even to the user. Throwing stars, knives, short swords, all had their advantages, most of which she was able to exploit. The advantages of the nunchaku remained a mystery to her.

She wondered how Brynja managed to carry so many; their weight was a challenge for anyone. That was part of the other training in store, the teacher said. It involved the medallion Magan had stopped wearing. Its powers were frightening, yet Magan knew she must learn how to use them.

At the moment, however, she couldn't concentrate on anything.

Brynja clearly was not affected in the same way. Her calm demeanor was inhuman under the circumstances. Did she never break down? Did she never scream at the forces around her?

Magan held up her hand and backed away to sit on the stool she'd found in another house. No one else needed it, at least not right now, and she was tired of sitting on the floor. What happened to her people's furniture and other possessions meant to make life comfortable? It was possible they took everything with them, but it was unlikely. They never possessed the number of wagons and carts necessary to move so much. Even so, there was very little left in the village. Perhaps thieves took what was left behind. The gates had gaped open when she and Dzorin returned, making it easy for thieves.

"Focus, Magan."

Brynja's voice was soft as usual, but there was irritation in her tone. She worked so hard to teach her, and Magan felt guilty when she let her down. But her mind would not focus right then.

"I can't," she said and remained seated. The wind sounded too much like the voices of her people, especially on the night when the raiders stole Iah away. Until now, she had forgotten the screams and shouting in the darkness.

"You must ..." Brynja began, but suddenly shrugged and turned away.

Magan disliked disappointing her. She worked hard to please her by making progress in learning weaponry and mystical lessons, delving into her own psyche, learning how far she could go. Admittedly, it wasn't just to please her teacher. She needed to learn; it was the reason for her being here, after all— to teach her everything she could in the short amount of time. Every day now, she wondered how far away Dzorin and their people were. Not for the first time, she wondered if they possessed the will to return.

She imagined things returning to normal within the village walls. Iah on his dais in the temple. A new high priest giving her a hard time in place of the dead Amleth about her lack of faith in the gods. And Dzorin. How would he feel about her once everything and everyone were in their accustomed places? When they left Sharvik in search of their god, they weren't friends, much less lovers. Their affection grew over the weeks and months of working and fighting together, of lonely nights, sometimes without a fire to keep them warm.

Would being among their people change him back to the man he was before that fateful night?

In the weeks since he left, she didn't thought of him as often as she expected. The lessons, Brynja's presence, distracted her. The medallion, the properties of which she had not yet been taught, the weapons, her words filled the days and dreams. She was right. There was too much to learn to sit idle.

"I am ready," she said, a bit more loudly than she intended. Brynja turned back toward her and nodded. Even she recognized the resolve in Magan's voice. However, instead of picking up the sword, Brynja pulled out the medallion with its colored stones.

"This is the right time, I think, to begin learning how to use this."

Magan suddenly felt short of breath. This was one of the things she hoped for, but seeing the firelight reflect from the stones brought memories of magical fights and disappearing people. Slowly, she rose and fetched her own medallion from the niche where she kept it, since she stopped wearing it on the chain around her neck after her earlier experience.

Brynja turned her own medallion lying in the palm of her hand, letting the light from the fire play across the stones. "This is what makes it possible to move without being seen. This is what your Friya used and helped the raiders to disappear, only to reappear somewhere else. There are many paths open through the magic of the stones."

"Can one become lost?" She'd asked the same question the first time. Although the answer was essentially, "No," she was still afraid.

"If one is not careful. If one does not learn what the sequences mean. There are shortcuts, crooked paths, but they can be dangerous. The straight paths are the safest."

Magan held her own medallion toward the firelight. This was what she longed to learn yet feared at the same time. Her power to move things, sometimes to listen to others' thoughts, those skills required great concentration, although Brynja taught her tricks to make it easier. Such powers could not compare to this.

"You must learn the magic of the medallion is not to be used lightly. The effects are profound and can be permanent. It should only be used in the most serious circumstances. Moving through the tunnels drains life force from living things the longer they remain there. There are ways to trap a person in a tunnel. There are ways to move large loads, like the weapons I brought. Even as heavy as your Iah.

"The simplest paths are activated with three stones." She pressed three in succession and disappeared. In a moment, she reappeared in the same place.

She told Magan the sequence, and she pressed the stones in her own amulet. Instantly, she found herself in a tunnel with misty walls, empty this time. She froze, unwilling to believe the floor was solid or movement was not blocked. She pressed the same three stones and returned to her place by the fire.

"Is the return code always the same as the original?" she

asked, the fear of losing herself, shaking her confidence again.

"Always," Brynja said.

"This is how you came to me."

"Yes."

Excitement slowly grew within Magan. This could be such wonderful knowledge, a tool to help her and her people as they rebuilt their lives in Sharvik.

She held out the medallion. "Teach me more."

Over the next few days, they practiced with weapons during the day. In the evening, Magan learned more and more ways in which to use the medallion. How to move through space and time, to appear and disappear where and when she wanted. It was important to keep control of the medallion. Without it, once inside the tunnels, it was possible to become trapped. Once trapped inside, the forces within it drained a person's energy. There were other ways to accomplish the same.

They entered tunnels together, visited other parts of the known world, and times in the near future and past. Brynja warned her moving through time was much more of a challenge and should be considered only under certain conditions.

The past few days, she'd been distracted by the thought of Dzorin's return. Four months had passed; it could be any day now. There was still so much to learn, and she was torn between hoping for more time and wishing to see him again.

She and Brynja practiced with swords every day. Their strokes became smooth, their movements timed perfectly, as if in a dance. Rarely did one surprise the other, but it was still beneficial exercise. Repetition made every move come much more naturally: muscle memory. Brynja changed the routine regularly and added various weapons to their practice sessions nearly every day

"The more you practice, the more likely you are to experience the red haze," she said. It was clearly a most desirable goal to her.

At night, Brynja showed Magan how to increase her abilities with magic and using her mind to do things most people couldn't. Or they passed through tunnels using the medallions, Magan memorizing sequences of the stones to help her move from place to place.

Late this night, Brynja took her into one of the tunnels, ending with them in the middle of the camp of the sleeping villagers on their way home. Magan was delighted and moved among her people, careful to make no noise. There were snores and groans coming from those who slept on the ground, in makeshift shelters, and on wagons.

Everyone looked worn, their clothes dirty and torn. She could feel their dreams, how tired they were. She wished she could gather them all together and carry them through the tunnels to Sharvik. But there were too many reasons not to.

Finding Dzorin wrapped in his cloak, she knelt beside him where he lay on the ground under the stars, snoring softly. He looked so peaceful, so gentle. She leaned down and kissed his cheek, and disappeared as his eyelids fluttered.

CHAPTER 16

Dzorin listened to sand and dust beat against the makeshift tent as it shook and fluttered wildly. Conversation was impossible for the half dozen people sitting cross-legged on rugs and cloths spread on the ground. The top of the tent was a foot above their heads, and the people sat close together. Every so often, someone re-set one of the wooden pegs used to anchor the cloth.

The rags tied around the lower part of their faces kept much of the dust out of their mouths and noses, but not all. It was so fine, it sifted through almost any cloth, making their mouths feel gritty. They coughed from the grit in their throats and lungs. They rinsed out their mouths with water, then spit into a jar to be emptied later.

Dzorin worried about how the rest of the people were doing. The storm came quickly, and there wasn't much time to batten down. Everyone worked frantically, knowing the effects of a sandstorm which lasted more than a day, and this one promised to do just that. The wall of sand reached for leagues end to end, darkening the desert as it moved.

Small items banged around outside, a few hitting the cobbled-together tent. They'd used every tent they already had and put together more using every piece of cloth and carpet they possessed, keeping the covers low in hopes the wind would not be able to get under and tear them away.

Most of their smaller possessions were also under the tents, or as many as they could manage. Some things were left out in the wind to take their chances: the wagons and carts, of course, still full water barrels, jars of food, anything with enough weight to oppose the wind. The animals were corralled by the wagons and carts to prevent their running away.

As the villagers worked to save themselves and their remaining food and possessions, Dzorin told them the storm may have already hit Sharvik. It came from the general direction of the village, meaning they were close to home. Once the storm was over, it was a matter of a few days until they were within those protective walls. It was an attempt to cheer them, make them more steadfast in surviving the storm. Whether it worked or not, he couldn't tell.

Night fell and they sat propped against one another, trying to sleep in spite of the noise outside. Some managed better than others, and snoring could barely be heard above the wind.

"Sounds like it might be letting up," Julin said. He spoke loudly for the others to hear.

"Could be," Dzorin said. At the moment, it didn't sound much different than it had all night. The walls of the tent were growing lighter, indicating sunrise or ebbing of the storm or both.

It was several hours later the sounds of the wind lessened. Gradually, every head rose, everyone listened another few moments and the tent settled. The storm lasted more than a day and ended as abruptly as it began.

As eager as they were to leave their confinement, Dzorin and Julin warned the others to wait in the tent a little longer. The wind still blew, so sand and dust swirled all around. The air was full of it, making breathing difficult. In spite of the warning to wait, people squirmed until the opening was undone, then crawled outside on all fours.

Everyone moaned and cursed at the stiffness in their joints while rising to their feet with difficulty, even painfully for some, including Julin. They kept the masks tied around their faces, but the coughing increased as they stepped out. The air was grey with the dust and sand rising and falling in the air. Others emerged from other cocoons nearby.

Possessions littered the ground as far as the eye could see. It would take at least a day to gather everything in. Some things were gone forever, but it couldn't be helped.

Heads were counted, and everyone seemed to be in good shape except for Erish, wife of the carpenter. She had discovered she was pregnant before they left Hattushah. The dust left her coughing and breathless and with abdominal pains. When they resumed their trek, she would have to ride on one of the carts, in hopes of preventing a miscarriage. One of the midwives stayed beside her over the last of their journey.

After a quick consultation, it was decided they must leave the next day. Sharvik being within a few days' travel, they could send a party back to this area to search for lost items later. Right now, they were tired and needed to rest once they'd gathered their belongings in order to reach home as soon as possible.

The day was spent in feeding and watering the animals. They moved about like gleaners, picking up scattered items and finding their owners. At sundown, exhausted and with aching bodies, they slept soundly.

The next day dawned clear and bright. The circle was broken up, the line of march re-set. Garaf and his priests moved among the people, telling them it wasn't too late to turn back. The gods were warning them. As much as the villagers believed in Iah, and respected his representatives, they didn't listen. After weeks of travel, Sharvik was only days away. Perhaps a week.

Loose sand and dust rose from the ground as they moved out, but it was nothing compared to the height of the storm, when the air was thick with it. Eventually, it would settle, and the ground would return to the hard pack they were used to.

Their feet dragged and the pace was slow. Once legs and feet limbered up, the pace quickened. They were near home. Their long trek was nearly over. And Dzorin was eager to be with Magan again.

As he slept, he felt her lips touch his forehead. He woke and looked to find her, but it was only a dream.

CHAPTER 17

Sword practice went on for some time. Magan's mind and body were focused. She swung the sword and Brynja slipped under the blade and moved behind Magan. This was a new move, pulling Magan's concentration into a new direction. She turned, barely parried the next blow. Brynja swung rapidly in a manner totally unlike her. Magan countered every blow while she moved backward step by step. The teacher's sword and arms moved together as if they were one, blow after blow. The sword flew from Magan's hands, and her back pressed against the wall on one side of the square. Her breathing was rapid, her breast rising and falling against the tip of her teacher's sword.

Magan expected chastisement for not concentrating, and she was ready to accuse Brynja of not playing fair. Then she looked into those blue eyes and realized Brynja's vision was turned inward.

"Magan," she called, but her lips did not move. The voice was inside Magan's head.

They stood thus for several heartbeats. Was Brynja aware Magan was disarmed? The teacher would never knowingly harm her, but the sword point still pressed against Magan's breast.

"Brynja?"

In a moment, the teacher smiled, and the sword lowered.

"Was that …"

"Yes. It's been a while since it has happened."

"Did you know it was me?"

"Oh, yes. I tried to touch your mind."

"I heard your voice inside my head," she said, scarcely believing it. "Truly?"

"Yes, truly."

"You didn't see me."

"Not with my eyes. Not in the normal way."

They stared at one another, Magan trying to understand what happened and what it meant to her. For only a moment, she felt she was in danger. Her trust in Brynja was complete, but not knowing what was going on under such strange circumstances or how far this phenomenon might carry them gave her pause.

"I would not have harmed you," Brynja said. "I knew where I was and what was going on."

"You seemed to be in a trance."

She shook her head. "It's not so isolating," she said.

"Why did you stand there for so long then?"

"I didn't want to give it up. The feeling is so rare, so precious." She stopped, took hold of Magan's shoulders and looked deeply into her eyes. "You will do it someday."

"Maybe tomorrow," Magan said and grinned, still not sure she wanted to.

The teacher shook her head and stepped away. "I must leave soon."

"Why?"

"Your people are very close, perhaps a week away. I must be gone before they arrive."

"No! I've so much more to learn."

"I've taught you everything I can. It's a matter of practicing now."

"But you said it would take a lifetime! You can't leave."

Brynja shook her head. "A lifetime of practice and patience."

Magan broke free and ran down the street, her confusion and sadness echoing in the silence. Mixed emotions chased her, nipping at her heels as she ran, leaving her feeling as if she were a child who didn't get her way. The thought made her angry.

For most of her life everything stayed the same, was predictable. After Iah was stolen, everything changed. Her life. The village. People came and went. Suddenly, she longed for stability, to know what to expect from one day to the next.

The familiar streets and alleys turned into a strange maze and she became lost, running in circles, up and down, back and forth. She slowed, finding her way. Eventually, she managed to get back to the square. Brynja sat on the steps of the temple. She approached her teacher reluctantly.

Brynja's head raised. Tears shone on her cheeks, clearly seen from a distance. She wiped them away with her sleeve and she stood as Magan approached. They fell into each other's arms.

"I love you," Magan said with a catch in her voice.

"I know."

"You can't leave me."

"I must. Your destiny does not lie with me. It is Dzorin with whom you must share the future." She took hold of Magan's arms and gently pushed her away.

"Dzorin." Magan spoke his name in anguish. The sound formed strangely on her lips. He would be back soon. She had missed him before becoming engrossed in learning, practicing. Feelings of guilt swept through her.

The love she felt for the older woman was not the chaste affection felt for a teacher or friend. She wanted nothing more than to go with her, spend time with her, know her. Loving someone else was a reminder of how she once was terribly angry with Dzorin for his feelings for Kira. But he was bewitched by magic. Brynja had not seduced her; falling in love the second time was as natural as the first. She reached out and touched the older woman's cheek with her fingertips.

"You must never tell Dzorin of your feelings for me."

"And what of yours for me?"

Brynja looked down to hide the emotion in her face. Magan wondered why she realized only now what was happening between them. It was her fault Brynja was in pain.

"He must never know any of this." Brynja ignored the question. "Magan, I am much older than you, and I'm bound to another. Dzorin is better suited to you. You still love him."

It was true. She loved him.

Magan brushed tears from Brynja's cheeks and walked away. Calmer now, she made her way through the gateway. Walking along the bank of the Diyala, memories of Friya and her alter ego, Kira, came to mind. How insulted, even frightened, she had been when Friya meant to seduce her when she first entered the high priestess's palace in Mari. In her village culture, such a relationship was forbidden, but in their travels, and in other encounters and conversations, she came to realize love and affection could not be controlled.

Later, as Kira, Friya seduced Dzorin. Magan was hurt and angry when he fell so hard. His later apologies and asking for understanding helped her to reconcile with him, realizing he was under a spell which he could not control.

Now, she was being taught it was possible to love two very different people at the same time. Something she thought impossible before.

There was nothing she could say. Her love for Brynja was strong, and a piece of her would be gone when the teacher left. At the same time, she loved Dzorin.

She sat on the edge of one of the ditches meant to carry water to the crops, dangling her feet in the dirt and sand. Dzorin and the others would return in a few days. What if his feelings were changed? What if the priests, the other warriors, the people, his own doubts, changed his mind? Made him believe their love was not meant to be? And without faith in Iah, she would drag him down?

Closing her eyes, she sought him in the distance. All she could sense was exhaustion and patience. Her own emotions were in the way, making concentration difficult.

Levering herself up, she walked slowly back into the village. Brynja waited in the house where they had spent many hours together. The weapons were gone, except for the katana which Magan now knew came not only from a different place, but from a different time.

Neither spoke again until later in the night, after they ate and the sun sat just above the horizon, leaving the streets in darkness, the top edges of higher buildings touched by light. The darkness of the night was gloomier than ever in spite of the fire in the fireplace.

Thus far, it was natural to sleep in the same room. Sharing the space made it feel warm and comfortable. This and the temple, where they went for practice and training, were the only two buildings they used.

After revealing their feelings for one another, Magan feared it might be awkward now. Instead, they felt more as though they both wanted to be together as much as possible during the last few days and nights.

They ate and talked of their separate lives, sharing memories and dreams.

"They depend on us to give them meaning," Brynja said. "Without us, they die."

Magan reached over and put a hand over her teacher's. They sat holding hands as they continued talking, until sleep overtook them. They lay down, their bodies melding together, and slept.

Brynja gathered up her belongings, preparing to leave. The weapons waited in one of the tunnels accessed with the medallion. Dzorin would arrive with the villagers in two days' time, she said.

The fire burned low and Magan stared into the embers. Their greater closeness for the past few days made parting more difficult even without the complication of loving one another. The lessons, the practice, everything they did further intertwined their minds and thoughts. Two people could gain insight into one another's minds. Concentrating on inner strength, on using her mind, brought Magan to near ecstasy. She did things she never dreamed anyone could do.

But there was so little time to work together on these strengths. Brynja guided Magan to them, letting her know what was possible. "You must reach out, learn what you can and can't do. You already know so much. Use what you know. Play, experiment. But remember, none of this should be used to further your own interests. These powers are not to make you rich or to achieve gratification, except in the service of others."

"And for my own preservation?"

"Yes, protect yourself by all means. And everyone who needs protection."

Magan stood, moved close to Brynja, touching her arm, running her hand up to her shoulder. She touched a scar there, then her fingers moved across her chest to the other shoulder. She ran her hand down the other arm. Brynja stood with eyes closed.

Magan's hand moved to her cheek. She traced the line of jaw to chin, moving to trace the lips, slightly parted. She leaned forward, touched her lips to the older woman's. Brynja looked down into her eyes. There were tears when she took Magan's hand.

"Magan …"

"Please."

"No," Brynja whispered.

Next morning, Magan went with her teacher to the gate and watched as the older woman walked away. Like Dzorin, Brynja didn't look back. Magan wanted to watch until she was out of sight, but her vision blurred and the lump in her throat threatened to choke her. It was too hard. When she was able to see, Brynja was gone. She used the medallion to move back to her own world. Walking away was a symbol of their parting to be remembered.

Where could Magan go? She walked the streets and alleys, returning to her own quarters to eat. There, she discovered the katana leaning in its scabbard against the wall of her sleeping space. Why would Brynja leave her most valued weapon? It was an extraordinary gift to any warrior, but Magan knew how much it meant to Brynja. Pray she found another one day. Magan lifted it, pulled the blade free, and sobbed.

For some time, she sat with the blade across her knees. Brynja's presence filled the room. Magan wavered between gladness and sadness; glad Brynja came into her life, sad to have lost her.

Growing restless after a time, she wandered toward the river where the water was at its usual low level. Stooping down, she examined one of the ditches, half-filled with dirt, the workings of the gates stiff from lack of use. Soon, the fields would be planted again, the water would flow, and her people would eat, drink, and be merry. Dzorin and she—

What would they do? Would they marry? Would they even be able to live peaceful lives in a village which may have grown too small for them after so many exotic adventures?

She turned and looked at the gate, the walls of the only home she ever knew. It was difficult to imagine a peaceful life, lived entirely within those walls. Becoming a wife, bearing children, settling into a normal life. Normal for other women. For her, it was always impossible. She wanted so much more of life.

Magan walked back into the village, leaving the gates open this time to welcome her people.

CHAPTER 18

Magan stood in the gateway, the midday sun beating down on her. The band of people topped the second hill, moving toward Sharvik purposefully. She watched for some time, knowing since early in the morning they would arrive today.

When first sighted, Garaf and his entourage led the way. As they drew nearer, others moved to either side of their large wagon. Some faces showed eagerness, others expressed joy, while others looked so relieved. Their journey was over.

She'd slept little the last two nights. Loneliness and dread overwhelmed her after Brynja left. She had wandered the streets, searching for the peace she usually felt when alone. It was only when she became involved with people her spirit was in such flux, and a lot of people were coming.

A figure separated from the crowd, running toward her. For a moment, she imagined another figure walking away.

Dzorin drew near and her pulse quickened. Memories of fearing for his safety, caring for him, loving him, his touch, took precedence over all else. Brynja was right.

She abandoned all pretenses, all guilt, and ran to meet him. He was back and she could face anything.

The first week, Magan and Dzorin helped everyone settle back into their homes, unloading carts and wagons, placing what possessions they still had in their proper places. Some of their own things were found and returned to them. Magan and Dzorin, above all others, appreciated the presence of people—friends and relatives—once more inhabiting Sharvik and she forgot the dread she felt before. The sounds of laughter, bickering, and simply living made them smile at one another often. The village was old and the silence within those walls felt heavy. They had not liked the weight of it.

Dzorin asked the first night if she found her teacher.

"Yes," she answered. "Her name was Brynja. She came from far away and was unlike anyone else we have ever known."

She described her and showed him the katana, let him feel its weight, how easy it was to wield. It was longer than their bronze swords, but he was so skilled it took him only a few swings to find its balance and know its reach. He handed it back in awe.

"It's a wonderful blade," he said.

She volunteered no further details, and he asked no questions. She didn't realize her sense of loss was clear in her voice until he squeezed her hand in understanding. Instead of pushing for more details, he told of his adventures during the months they were separated, beginning with finding the villagers in squalid conditions outside Hattushah. He glossed over the preparations to leave but described the battle on the road home in detail, praising the other warriors, suggesting Crosus might still seek revenge. He waited until the second day when they were alone in her house to tell her of Lahnlee.

"I should have told you about him right away, I suppose," he said. "It's just I haven't come to terms with his pain."

"It would seem he will never know where the body of his son lies," Magan said. "Should we leave him where he is now buried? Or should we bring his body here for burial?"

"The priests may not agree since Tarn was one of the raiders who stole Iah."

"We can postpone any decision until we dig them up," Magan said. She paused. "I'm sorry we caused him such pain since you say he was a very nice man. Maybe we'll find him again one day and explain."

She was familiar with Dzorin's empathy for others. He'd exhibited it to their detriment when they found Kira, the young persona adopted by Friya in the nomad's camp. His need to rescue her had less to do with any spell the witch cast than it did with his innate kindness.

They lay quietly for a time until she said, "You weren't the one who actually killed Lahnlee's son. Since the two of you became friends, we better tell Lahnlee it was my doing and you were just a witness. If we ever see him again."

Dzorin protested, but she insisted. He had not raised a hand against Tarn, although his participation wasn't innocent. Tarn's certainly was not. However, the chances of meeting the merchant again seemed slim, and the problems of settling their people were more immediate.

Homes must be swept clean, aired out, or repaired, the granary made ready, the irrigation ditches and gates repaired. It took more than a year for so much to fall into disrepair. In less than a month the fields must be ready for planting and the irrigation system repaired and re-organized to the point they could water the seeds they'd brought with them. Every hand was needed. Craftsmen repaired walls and gates, everyone took a hand at sweeping. Children carried material and women wove and sewed. Metal hinges were sanded and lubricated. Stables and corrals for the animals were rebuilt.

Every person performed their tasks, some learned new skills working beside artisans. Several of the priests helped everywhere, although Garaf and the few closest to him held themselves aloof from the mundane work. Julin wore himself out every day, encouraging everyone, helping everywhere.

Erish gave birth prematurely to a baby girl. Both mother and daughter suffered no ill effects, except Erish took a little longer than usual to recover. It was also unusual for so many people to be in attendance at a birth, but after she nearly lost the baby on the trek, they all felt part of the event.

Garaf chided Varas for the delay in recovering Iah. Without the idol, everything was meaningless, he said. However, the villagers continued to work, saying among themselves having food and a place to sleep was just as necessary. However, they must soon bring god back to his village waiting to receive him.

A week passed, and everything became more normal. Water ran into the fields from the river or was carried there in buckets since the river was down. The spring thaws had passed, but there should be plenty of water for the planting. The yield from the seeds would be smaller, true, but with the food they brought, and the lentils and beans stored in jars, they would survive.

The ground was worked and seeds were planted. Onions and garlic would grow well into the autumn. Water would have to be carried to some parts of the fields, of course. With what they could grow and the foodstuffs they brought with them, they would survive to plant another season.

Dzorin and Magan met with Varas, Julin and others to plan for the trip to retrieve Iah from his burial place. They had not told anyone a man was buried with the god, and he and Magan decided it wasn't necessary to do so beforehand.

"I wish for only one thing," Dzorin said one night.

Magan snuggled against him in the now friendlier darkness. They had become accustomed to sleeping in her house since it sat nearer the central courtyard than his.

"What?"

"That we could marry."

"When?"

"Tomorrow. The day after. Soon."

"You know we can't until Iah is back in place."

"I know." He sighed. "Not until then will they name a high priest, and so on."

She laughed softly. "There's no hurry. We've done well so far."

"Yes."

He turned onto his side to face her and ran his fingertips over her body. Since his return, they'd made love almost every night, making up for lost time, he said. This night, though, they were both too tired. Even so, his touch stirred her passion.

She lay enjoying the closeness and the knowledge their village was once more populated as it should be. Brynja was right: there was no need to tell Dzorin of the unconsummated feelings between them. Having learned the lesson was enough. Soon Iah would be returned to his temple, and all would be right with their world.

"Have you noticed how some of the women watch us when we're together?" Magan asked.

"Not just them. A couple of the other warriors could hardly keep their jaws from dropping."

"Everything has changed so much." Magan sighed. "Most things I would not turn back. It all just happened so fast."

Dzorin laughed softly. "It's approaching two years."

"Yes, but compared to all the years before …" She yawned.

He pulled her closer as he began to fall asleep, and she relaxed to do likewise.

"Where did your teacher come from?" Dzorin asked, his voice low.

Surprised, Magan took a moment to answer. "She wouldn't say."

"Oh."

"It was far away, though. Her name and accent were so different." She realized something strange: Brynja and she understood each other's speech. Oh, there were strange words mixed in, but they were no impediment to understanding each other.

Dzorin kissed her, seeming to be satisfied with the answer. Soon his regular breathing told her he was asleep. Magan lay awake for a long time. No matter how right Brynja had been, Magan couldn't help feeling a little guilt, not because she loved Brynja but because she could not tell Dzorin. Her feelings and reaction to Dzorin's infatuation with Kira were past, although she wondered if he completely forgave her for killing the woman he thought he loved. She forgave him long ago for loving another but had not forgotten. Maybe it was enough. But if she did tell him about Brynja, he would know she now understood better what happened.

Anyway, she couldn't tell him tonight. He was asleep.

The days became busier as they gathered together the things needed for the trek to the dry riverbed in between helping with the work of restoring life to Sharvik. Weapons and tools were cleaned and sharpened. Clothes were mended and replaced, food and water set aside. One of the wagons was commandeered, along with a pair of oxen to pull it.

Magan and Dzorin went over the route, trying to remember every landmark along the way. Some things would have changed, of course, given the passage of time. However, the desert was eternal and neither doubted they could find the right spot. The events were forever part of their memories, part of whom they had become.

So much about them was changed, not the least being their falling in love when, in the beginning, they could barely tolerate one another. Because of their relationship, people now looked at Magan differently, as if Dzorin's affection for her made her a different—a better—person. They would never accept her as fully as they did Dzorin, but perhaps the time of overt discrimination was over.

A month passed and finally everyone was satisfied the village was near what it should be. The trek to Iah's burial place was planned. Garaf was asked if he wanted to go with the group but he declined. Nor would he send one of the priests with them. In a particularly cruel decision, he forbade even Julin from going. The priest was terribly disappointed, but he couldn't go against the command of his superior.

The night before they left, Magan and Dzorin fell into bed early, exhausted by the day's work in readying everything for the next day when the party was to start out at daybreak. Neither of them slept for a while, too worked up to relax, but pretended to so as not to disturb the other. The culmination of a year-and-a-half of struggle was just hours away.

Finally falling asleep, Iah came to her again in a dream. He lay in the hole in the sand of the riverbed, partially exposed, sunshine gleaming from the golden surface, obscuring his face until she got closer. She sat on the edge of the hole, her feet dangling near the god's side. It did not startle her when his eyes opened; she expected it.

"You are coming at last," he said. His lips did not move; the words were in her head.

"Yes, soon."

"Stay alert. My return to the village will not be any easier than your finding me."

She laughed. "Nothing has been easy thus far. Why would this be different?"

"Why, indeed? The world is a dangerous place, as you've discovered, and you will find no peace in it."

"Am I condemned for some reason? Why would peace elude me? Us?"

"You have always longed to live a life far removed from the ordinary lives of your people. You haven't learned to be careful what you wish for."

His eyes closed, and she sat for several minutes looking down at the idol, as wide as it was tall. Sand covered most of the base and one arm. Why would their god talk to her, an unbeliever? A doubter? Yet he did on several occasions, if these dreams and visions were more than childish imaginings. Maybe her own feelings of guilt created these illusions. Even if true, she would keep his words of warning in mind.

Most of the villagers gathered in the courtyard outside the temple to see the party off. Garaf refused to appear, showing disapproval because it took so long to retrieve Iah. Most of the priests joined the others. Julin blessed the oxen, the wagon, the party heading out, and the people gathered to watch. The atmosphere was celebratory and expectant.

Magan and Dzorin warned everyone it would take longer to reach the site than on their original trek when they were unencumbered and moved faster. This time, they were a larger group, plus the wagon and oxen. Once the weight of the idol was added to the wagon, the return would take even longer. The people ignored the warnings, most of them refusing to accept they must wait so much longer, perhaps even as much as two or three weeks. Julin promised those leaving he would not let the villagers' spirits wane.

Five warriors joined Varas, Dzorin, and Magan as they set out in the early morning darkness, unable to hide their own eagerness. The day was already warm since spring rapidly turned into summer. The two oxen pulled the best wagon available, blessed again by Julin as they passed through the open gateway. He had become so indispensable many whispered they hoped he might become high priest, although everyone knew it wasn't possible. Nearly all those staying behind followed to the gates, wishing them success and a speedy return. Arms waved gaily until the party moved out of sight.

In many ways, everything was very similar to the other morning, months ago, when Magan and Dzorin set off in the same direction. Being well-armed and wearing the same attire as before gave a feeling of renewal, and events were finally coming full circle. She also felt a strange discontent for which she could find no reason, and she marked it down to nerves.

CHAPTER 19

They reached the dead village easily enough. It took eleven days at a relatively easy pace instead of seven as the cart and ox could not travel as fast as the two of them had alone. There was also a trail to follow the first time.

They looked down on the structures, more derelict than before, much as Magan and Dzorin did the first time, except this time in the light of midday instead of evening. It looked much the same: abandoned.

No smoke rose into the air, no voices filled the silence, broken only by wind blowing through and between the structures. Sand was piled higher against the walls. Stones had fallen from atop a wall here and there. An overall dusty appearance warned further of the desert's reclaiming the land on which the mud-brick walls stood.

Without a word, the two led the way down the hill. The first time, they found bodies in the square around the well in the center, a few lay inside just as they fell to the swords of the raiders the two were following. She suspected none of the bodies or bones would be there now. Scavengers would have cleaned it out pretty well, yet she couldn't help a sense of dread of what they might find.

They emerged from between two structures into the open square, the homes and workshops forming four sides around it. Sand drifted against the fronts of the buildings on one side, partially blocked the doorways. The raiders took everything of any value.

Dzorin moved right and Magan moved left toward the well, along the same paths as before. No sense of human habitation came to her, not even of death. Piles of charred bits of wood indicated travelers had passed through, stopping to light fires to keep warm or to heat food.

She leaned against the rock wall of the well and looked down. Cooler air drifted up, smelling of damp. The jug and rope were gone, possibly taken by nomads. She picked up a small stone from the ground and dropped it in the well. Its splash in the water came back quickly, indicating the water was still high and accessible if they could rig something to lower inside. Five skins were still full, enough to last for days, but it was always a good idea to refill the empty ones when the opportunity presented itself. She regretted not bringing water jugs, which would have been easier to manipulate in the well, but they were heavier to carry.

She watched Dzorin enter one of the buildings, feeling dread at what might be encountered inside. She turned back to her study of the well when a yell came from behind her. Cail burst from another building, followed closely by a hyena, snapping at his heels. Magan yelled and waved her arms, startling the animal. It halted suddenly and turned toward her, its lips drawn back, revealing sharp teeth. She drew her sword slowly while returning the animal's stare. To one side, she caught Cail's movement as he turned with drawn sword. From the left, another figure approached. She sensed it was Leod.

"Let's get it," Cail said tightly, and the hyena crouched.

"Wait," Magan ordered. "It's outnumbered. They're cowards. Maybe it will just run away."

Everyone stood very still, the hot sun beating down. Sweat ran down Magan's sides from the heat and tension as she tried to touch the creature's mind. *Run away*, she thought to it. Just as it seemed she could stand there no longer, the hyena threw back its head and laughed in its maniacal way. The next moment, it sprang for the shade between two buildings and was gone. Everyone relaxed with loud exhalations and coughs. Magan watched as the animal trotted out of the village and out of sight across a dune while the others went about their explorations. After several minutes passed with no sign of the beast or any others, she too relaxed, confident the hyena was no longer a threat.

She set Leod to the task of rigging up one of their empty waterskins with a cord to see if they could draw water from the well, then went in search of Dzorin. With all the noise during the fracas, he hadn't reappeared.

She passed into the shade of the house she'd seen him enter. Furniture and other possessions still lay strewn about the floor, although fewer than before. Not surprising, given the charred remnants in the courtyard. A layer of dust covered everything. Footprints led into the next room. Magan stepped through and spotted Dzorin in the far-right corner. She raised her hand and opened her mouth to speak then stopped short.

He stood absolutely still, eyes wide, his gaze fixed on something on the floor she couldn't see from her position. His fear beat against her mind. Carefully, she drew the katana from the scabbard slung across her back. Edging around, trying not to make a sudden noise, she scanned the broken jumble of items for what could cause Dzorin to be so afraid. She shifted position and brushed against a small table lying on its side. Dzorin's eyes widened when it rocked against another piece, making a slight sound.

She crept around a broken table. The interior twilight showed only shadows of the flotsam. She eased down to sit on her heels and leaned backward to balance herself against the wall. Carefully, she examined every stick and shred, using both eyes and mind. Primitive life lay concealed there. She felt its presence, its fear. Then she saw it. One of the sticks flicked its tongue outward, tasting the air. Dzorin had disturbed a viper. One bite would prove fatal, and it was poised to strike.

Her hands were moist and she wanted to wipe her palms on her tunic. Fear—the snake's, Dzorin's and now her own—swept over her.

She took a slow, deep breath and surveyed the surroundings. There was no way to get at the serpent through the rubble with her sword. It was protected above and on all sides by debris, and fearfully close to Dzorin. There was a chance the snake would eventually leave if they stayed perfectly still; it was their best chance.

"Magan," someone yelled from the outer door. "Dzorin."

Broken furniture rattled and the sound of footsteps moved across the first room. The snake's head rose. In slow motion, it struck forward. With a shout, Magan smashed downward with her sword. She could hear Dzorin's yell as if echoing from deep in the ground. Her arms moved painfully slowly in their downward arc. The sword cut through debris, scattering it, and jarred against the dirt floor. The vibrations rattled her arms.

"Magan, what's wrong?" It was Leod's voice, bringing her back to real time.

She blinked and looked at her sword. The snake's head lay on one side of the blade, the mouth opened wide, revealing the fangs poised to bite, its writhing body on the other side. The sword's sharp edge pressed into the dirt.

Her mouth was dry, and she tried to swallow. Moving only her eyes, she looked up at Dzorin, who crouched so near the snake he could reach out to touch the head. It was the last thing he would do. Beads of sweat shone on his forehead. Air exploded from his lungs, and he slumped against the wall. He looked at her and smiled and touched his upper arm where the amulet would have been were it not lost during their adventures.

He'd worn one since birth, to ward off the fate settled on him. As he grew, up, a new one was made to fit him better. It was deemed his death would be caused by the bite of a snake. Dzorin's amulet was lost months ago when they were captured and enslaved and neither of them gave it a thought since. At least, she hadn't.

She didn't believe in supposed portents, since they were meant to make it possible for the priests to sell the amulets. She accepted he believed it, and knew it was best not to mention her doubts about amulets and priestly predictions at the moment.

"We better get out of here," he said.

He rose and walked stiffly to her and held out his hand. Her knees shook slightly as they walked arm in arm from the building, a puzzled Leod following. As soon as they were able to talk calmly, Magan and Dzorin told him what happened.

"Sorry. I didn't know."

"It wasn't your fault, Leod." Magan patted his arm. "You had no way of knowing, and there was no time to tell you."

"I should have been more prepared for such dangers," Dzorin said. "But the village was so deserted the first time."

"The people had only been dead for a day or two, remember?"

"What about Sharvik? Have you wondered why no animals moved in there while it was deserted?"

"There were no bodies to draw them?" Magan said.

"Some might still have gone in looking for shelter or just checking it out."

"I guess it is curious." She turned to Leod. "Did you need us for something when you came inside?"

"Oh, yes. We managed to get some water from the well and were wondering if you wanted to stay long enough to fill all of the empty skins."

"How many are still empty?"

"Three. It's taking a while drawing with a skin."

"I think we should fill them all, just in case. Dzorin?"

"We might as well. We could get more leagues out of the way before dark, but it won't hurt to sleep here, instead."

Reaction was starting to set in, and Magan felt a need for action. However, everything was being done. A walk would help settle mind and body. She moved off to inspect the doorways of the other buildings, and Dzorin joined her.

"We should send people back here to take whatever furniture we can repair and use," she said. "It would be a shame to let it sit here and dry rot."

"We could add some of it to the cart when we return this way," he said.

She nodded, and they walked in silence again.

"You could have been killed," she said after several moments. Her voice shook with the fear of what might have happened. "I was so afraid. I didn't know what to do." Her voice grew slightly shrill.

He put an arm around her shoulders. "I know," he said. "It could have turned on you. Crouched down as you were, there was no chance of getting clear."

"I sensed he didn't know I was there."

"You can sense animals?"

"A little. Not like people, though." They walked in silence for a time. "What if I wasn't fast enough?"

"You were. Everything is all right."

He stopped, put his arms around her, holding her close. The shaking stopped after a few minutes. She looked up into his face, and he gave her a quick kiss. They turned and walked on.

"I've faced men with swords," Magan said. "We just encountered a hyena a few minutes earlier. In our travels, there were many other dangers. I don't think I've been more frightened than I was back there with the snake."

He laughed. "Because you love me," he said teasing.

"Yes, I do. And don't you ever take such a risk again."

She poked him in the ribs and took off running with him close behind.

CHAPTER 20

"There's a man buried with Iah. One of the warriors who attacked Sharvik." Dzorin spoke matter-of-factly.

The men's eyes went wide, and they looked at him, at each other, and murmured amongst themselves. He and Magan watched their faces, shining in the light of the fire in the center of their circle. All of the waterskins were filled and they sat around a fire of wood scrounged from the surrounding buildings.

"Why didn't you tell us earlier?" Cail asked.

"We were afraid you might not want to come with us," Magan answered.

"You didn't trust our dedication to get Iah back to Sharvik?"

"After everything our people have been through in the past year, we were simply afraid this last thing, what many people would see as desecration, might be seen as too ill an omen," Dzorin explained.

He and Magan had discussed telling the men. She told him of the dream about Iah's being exposed to view. There was nothing in the dream of the man's body, leading her to think they must not speak of it very . Now, she was afraid she was mistaken.

"We didn't mean to keep anything important from any of you," she said. "It just didn't seem to ever be the right time, nor did we have the right words to tell you. Even after such a long time, the memory still gives us both nightmares."

Dzorin recounted the details, substituting the man cutting his own throat with Magan's doing it for him. The other warriors looked at her with new respect. He told of their strength of desperation, allowing them to lift the idol, pull the ropes around it, and drag it from the tent to the dry riverbed. When he finished, Cail shrugged.

"You had no choice," he said. "Saving Iah and yourselves was the most important thing."

"Garaf and the priests might not agree," Varas said. "It's best we keep this to ourselves."

Everyone spoke at once, some speaking for, some against what Varas suggested. Their voices dropped out one at a time until all were silent.

"We wanted you to know what you might find once we start digging," Dzorin said, "and to know we meant no sacrilege. The priests may have to come to terms with what happened. Perhaps some cleansing ceremony."

"Phaw!" Cail said. "We don't have to tell them. What they don't know ..." He shrugged.

Everyone looked around the circle, gauging whether all of them could, or would, keep such a thing secret. Magan and Dzorin eventually moved away from the rest, letting them talk freely amongst themselves, coming to terms with what they just learned.

"They're taking it better than I thought they would," Magan said.

"I dreaded telling them," Dzorin said. "Now all we have to worry about is how the rest of the village will take it."

"If we have to make it known."

She reached over and patted his hand. "We may not have to if they agree to say nothing about it." She nodded toward the group nearer the fire. "Whatever they decide, we will all have to live with. What can Garaf do? Refuse to take him back?"

"Not him. Us."

It was not a new thought, but Dzorin's voicing the fear made it more real.

The discussion lasted only a short time, and the two returned to the fire with their comrades. It was agreed no one else need know about the circumstances of Iah's burial. Questions were asked about the finding of Iah; Isik wanted to know more about his friend Vanthi, who died later. Dzorin told of how the three of them were on their way back to Sharvik when they became trapped by a flood in a canyon. Of how the two of them searched and could not find any trace.

Isik recounted his injuries and Vanthi's continuing along the trail they had followed. After one day trying to work his way back to Sharvik, he became so weak, he lay down to die. He woke in a tent belonging to a woman — a widow — who nursed him back to health. He stayed with her for ten days and admitted he regretted leaving her.

"Once everything is settled in Sharvik, I intend retracing my steps to find her. Her people support her, but she needs a man."

The others kidded him at the same time they pledged to help him find the way. Varas chided him for not telling them before.

More stories were told of similar adventures while they were away trying to find where Iah was taken. The disappearing trails. They talked well into the night, finally drifting off to lie down wrapped in their rugs and blankets.

Magan and Dzorin lay next to each other in the darkness. She watched the stars set against the blackness. She was almost afraid to go to sleep, afraid of what she might dream about.

Several more days of travel brought them to the riverbed; it was too late in the day to do any digging, but Magan and Dzorin examined the sandy surface trying to determine the exact location of the burial. Nothing distinctive in the area indicated where the idol was buried, although not much was changed. Not long ago, water flowed down from the mountains, probably from the spring thaws and distant rains, scrubbing the sand into the same featureless landscape. Unlike in her dream, the golden figure was not visible.

Sighting on the flat area where the raiders' camp had been, they determined the general area of the burial. Only by digging several test holes would they be able to pinpoint it.

Work started next morning. Two holes were begun, ten feet apart, with two men working together on each. Magan paced anxiously, afraid she and Dzorin had misjudged. Although, it was in this general area, searching the sand for any telltale marks proved useless. On the night of the burial, the spot was selected in the dark, in a hurry, and the hole dug. Afterward, they did their best to conceal the spot. They both knew this was the riverbed; the large campsite was one hundred feet away and higher. They sighted from the rocks where they hid until the camp went to sleep. They stepped out the perimeter of the camp, the location of the tent, sighted from there, then stepped out the distance from the riverbank.

Nothing prepared them for the frustration of searching for the burial site, and not finding it. They all took turns digging, and the holes expanded.

Magan opened her mouth to suggest they move to another spot. The wooden hoe Leod was using struck something hard, and he stopped. The sound was heard by all. He looked at her with an expression of hope.

"Dzorin," she called.

He turned from watching the second digging operation.

"We've hit something."

The other two men stopped digging. Everyone gathered as Leod discarded the hoe and used his bare hands to clear away sand so as not to damage the idol they hoped was found at last. Although dry as a bone, the sand was hard-packed, so the digging was difficult. No one offered to help since the space was small, and Leod was the one who struck the object. It was his to uncover.

As Leod worked, the sheen of gold shown through, grew until finally, all could see. With the bulk of the idol slightly to the right of where he had been digging, he moved over slightly.

"Cail," Leod called to his friend. "Take the sand from the top there." He indicated the undisturbed surface from the edge of the hole.

Cail nodded and began clearing away the top level with his hoe. Leod pushed sand from around the exposed side of the idol with his fingertips. Magan watched intently, fingers itching to get at the sand, but she held herself in check. Dzorin glanced at her, and she saw the same desire in his eyes. She nodded curtly, then both returned their attention to the growing golden surface.

Before long, one side and the head of the idol were cleared, and the two men began working on the opposite side. The idol showed no damage from its burial. It still lay on its back, its sightless eyes staring up into the late afternoon sky. For an instant, those eyes opened and stared at her. She looked around at the others. Had anyone else seen? Was she the only one? Magan closed her own eyes and rocked back on her heels, nearly falling backward. Dzorin put an arm around her, a quizzical look on his face. She smiled to reassure him.

Cail stopped working, looked around at the expectant faces.

"You can help anytime now," he said.

Everyone laughed and began digging with hoes and shovels, enlarging the hole. Magan stepped back, giving them plenty of room, no longer aching to help. Dzorin also lost his need to uncover the idol, although enthusiasm glowed in his face. The people of Sharvik would thrive again. Belief was the magic of Iah and other gods. Belief in them supported lives, dreams, even decisions. The end of the long journey was within a few feet, a few moments.

The chattering stopped. Magan approached the hole. Dzorin came up beside her and took her hand. At their approach, the men looked up and moved apart so the two could see. Lying partially uncovered next to the golden body lay the remains of Tarn. The skin was wrinkled and tight like parchment. The dark hair stood up on his head. A sword lay close to the dry fingers. Instead of decaying, his body was dried out in the arid sand.

"It will be easier to free Iah if we remove the body first," Leod said.

Everyone nodded agreement, but not one person moved.

"I'll do it," Magan said quietly.

Dzorin started to say something, but she held up her hand.

"I killed him and placed his body there. I will move him out of the way."

"It will be much appreciated," a voice said from the bank.

All eyes turned.

"Lahnlee!"

The old man glared at Dzorin. "I've come to claim the body of my son and avenge his murder."

"How did you know ..." Dzorin began.

Lahnlee turned from him to contemplate the hole, the golden idol, and the body of his son.

"It wasn't murder," Dzorin said.

"He is dead," he said without looking away. "His body will be burned after the traditions of my people."

"Dzorin," Magan whispered. "He's not alone."

Dzorin looked beyond Lahnlee. "I don't see ..."

"I feel ... a presence," she whispered.

Magan said the last word with distaste. A shudder seized Dzorin.

"Friya?" he asked.

"Yes. Behind him somewhere."

"That's how he knew."

A figure moved from behind the merchant to stand at his side, staring like him at the burial. Then she turned to look full into Magan's eyes. The suddenness was meant to catch Magan off guard, to intimidate her, but the younger woman was no longer as unsure of her abilities or strengths. And her own hatred was as strong as the witch's.

Friya's appearance was of the high priestess, neither young nor old, the woman who enslaved her and meant to sacrifice her in the arena of Mari. Magan first saw her in this guise before seeing the old and haggard witch whose cruelties were reflected in her face. It was the same Friya whose seduction Magan resisted. Lastly, she'd seen her as Kira, the young seductress who stole Dzorin's affections in revenge for Magan's rejection, finally, the witch who took the form of a dragon in their final battle.

In their escape from Mari, Magan had battled all three of them, one after the other, and still Friya was alive. It might not be possible to kill her, but Magan now knew she possessed the means to conquer her.

Another figure appeared and stood behind Friya. Magan recognized one of the white-skinned guards from the high priestess's palace.

"We are ready, My Lady."

"They are all yours except the girl." The eyes continued to glare at Magan. "Lahnlee, the order is yours to give."

Magan glanced at Dzorin. He quietly drew his sword, and she could hear the other warriors of Sharvik scrambling out of the hole slightly behind. Two of their men moved quickly across the sand to where their weapons lay, returned to their comrades and handed them out. What would be Friya's weapon of choice, or would she prefer to match strength another way?

Magan drew the katana from its scabbard for the first time in anger. The only time during their trek it was uncovered was in the dead village. The rest of their trip, it lay in the wagon, wrapped in cloth to protect it. Once they reached the riverbed, the steel sword was kept close, for what reason she wasn't sure. She carried it at the burial site due to some instinct. Now she prepared to defend herself.

More men appeared behind the witch and climbed down the bank, surrounding the smaller group. They wore clothes and armor like those of the party which raided Sharvik more than a year before and stole Iah, the warriors who disappeared somewhere in this desert. They were not of Mari, although the witch employed many among her private guards. Several wore medallions on chains around their necks.

Based on what she learned from Brynja, they came from a land out of this time, out of this place. A land from which they came to lure Tarn to his death and Lahnlee to avenge his death and now claim his son's body. The turns of time and events were crossing each other in strange patterns. Brynja said it was sometimes this way.

"Stay close," Dzorin muttered.

Magan nodded but knew Dzorin could not protect her from Friya's hatred, nor could Magan protect him. He must fight with the men as a warrior. She must fight alone as the woman she was now. Now she would know whether she was strong enough.

CHAPTER 21

"I killed your son, Lahnlee," Magan said. "None of these men were here when Tarn died."

"Dzorin was here," Lahnlee said.

"Yes, he was. But he took no part in Tarn's death."

"He was there," he repeated.

"These other men were not."

"They are here now," Friya spoke up. She addressed Magan's companions. "Will you give up the body and the idol?"

"No! Not Iah." The voice from behind was Varas's. "You may take the body and be damned."

"Then you will all die." The high priestess motioned to someone else behind her. Another white guard stepped forward. Friya pointed to Magan.

"She's the one. Be careful of any tricks."

More soldiers appeared behind her, seeming to step out of a hidden doorway, joining the group clustered in the riverbed, numbering twelve in all. Magan kept her attention on Friya and the guard standing at the witch's side.

Around her, warriors rushed together, blades reflecting light from the sun. Shouts rose, metal rang against metal. The men of Sharvik were outnumbered. She knew they were determined to return Iah to his place in Sharvik. In addition, they wanted to avenge his loss and their humiliation. Would all such determination be enough for victory? Was it too much to hope success might be theirs at last?

Physical and emotional violence pounded at her. She tried to block them, but there were so many, their fear and anger pushed through her mental barriers. Dzorin was hard-pressed by two of the huge warriors. Varas fought slowly, feeling his age, but with such skill, he kept his opponent at bay. Their emotions, and of the others, mixed with her own.

The white warrior jumped from beside Friya to the riverbed, his blood up. Magan shook her head to clear her mind of others' thoughts and waited, ready, full of remorse at this turn of events.

Why would Friya choose a champion to fight for her while she stood back, watching?

Friya's champion wore metal armor protecting the vulnerable parts of his body. It was heavy, but he lunged at her as if it weighed nothing. In moments, it was clear he was also a skilled swordsman, not depending on just his superior size to overcome his adversary. His style was careful, inexorable, wearing. His caution gave Magan credit for having skill with the sword. However, her skill was countered somewhat by the presence of Friya. Magan divided her concentration between guarding her mind as much as her body. The high priestess probed constantly, testing, seeking a way through her defenses.

Surprise, Friya. I am stronger than when we last met. You didn't expect that, did you?

No answer. Magan thanked Brynja for her teaching then dismissed the memory to keep Friya from hearing. If she knew of the teacher, she might know the pupil too well.

The white warrior slashed at her. Magan caught his blade with her own. She slipped underneath, attacking when he was turning. They exchanged several blows. She realized his purpose was to tire her, if not to kill her. Friya wasn't taking many chances.

Magan dodged a blow and ran a few steps beyond. With her free hand, she pulled the medallion from under her tunic. It hung heavily around her neck. She pressed the stones.

One moment, she prepared to counter another swing of the white warrior's blade, the next everything around her faded and she stood in the time passage, looking back at her mystified adversary. The witch and the warrior didn't expect her to have learned the power of the medallion. She touched the stones again, reappeared behind him.

"She has a medallion," Friya cried, as if the warrior hadn't already realized.

Caught by surprise, the warrior started toward her, bringing his weapon up in a defensive move. Magan drove the tip of the katana blade into a gap in the armor in the warrior's side. He grimaced and fell to one knee. Another swing and she cut his bare thigh to the bone. He cried out, crumpled to the ground. Magan kicked his sword away, wanting only to disable him. He tried to push himself to his feet.

"Stay down and I won't kill you," Magan said. "My fight is with your high priestess."

His breath came in panting gulps, matching her own. Their eyes locked on each other, and acceptance crept into his gaze. He lay back, exhausted by loss of blood and pain. He closed his eyes. There was no more fight left in him, only fear and pain. Magan nodded and turned to Friya, still watching from the higher ground.

"Well? It's you and me now, Friya."

The high priestess stood still, her gaze moving from the fallen warrior and back to Magan, contemplating her next move. As her mind raced over possible courses of action, the images played through Magan's mind.

"Another dragon, perhaps?" Magan asked.

Friya shook her head, startled at being overheard. She regained her composure quickly, still sure she could win. She pulled at the chain of the medallion around her neck.

"It might work this time," the high priestess said. "There's no fire for you to use against me as you did before."

In her encounter with the witch in her Kira form, Magan used the witch's own magical fire to defeat her.

"True. This time, though, I have a medallion." Once again, the witch's own magic.

Magan pressed the stones before Friya pressed her own. She ran along the tunnel, turned and watched Friya appear in the same spot. She had let the witch read her mind as she pressed the stones so she would know the route. They stood facing each other, Friya bombarding Magan with power, beating against the walls in her mind.

Dzorin saw Magan disappear. He let down his guard for an instant and the enemy Guardsman managed to nick his arm with a twitch of his sword. He didn't see Friya follow. Reluctantly, he focused on protecting himself from blows of the other's sword, while hoping Magan knew what she was doing.

Sounds of other warriors fighting for their lives surrounded him. For a moment, he caught a glimpse of Lahnlee standing on the riverbank watching grimly. The merchant's anger and hatred were so strong, even Dzorin could feel it. Instead of distracting him, the other man's anger added to his own.

It was impossible to keep it down. This was supposed to be the final step to settling everyone back into Sharvik, to everyone coming home. They needed peace to bring life back where it was before the nighttime raid. He cursed the gods and swung his sword harder. It was time to end this!

His focus narrowed to the man who strove to kill him. Dzorin stepped close, pushed the man in the chest, putting him off-balance. Dzorin's sword seemed to have a mind of its own, as it struck time and again, beating against the other's sword.

"Leave us alone," he said through gritted teeth.

The man tripped and fell and Dzorin finished him, driving the point of his sword into his chest. Blood burst from the man's mouth. Dzorin turned away from his death throes to engage another.

Varas was having a difficult time coping with the attacks of two of the white warriors. Dzorin rushed over and cut one man's heel from behind. He collapsed in a heap. His fellow warrior turned to see what happened and Varas caught him in the side with the tip of his sword. It plunged deeply into the body and he also crumpled as the captain pulled his blade free.

Dzorin looked around to see Leod go down, bleeding from a deep cut on his neck. He leaped toward the man who struck his friend and cut him down quickly. Varas rushed to help Cail who also struggled to defend against two.

For the first time, Dzorin realized Friya was also gone. Perhaps her disappearance was the reason her warriors appeared less than competent.

CHAPTER 22

Magan sheathed her sword and took a small doll carved from burdock Brynja showed her how to make. It was dressed in green cloth, meant to resemble the high priestess's gown. Magan carried it with her everywhere, knowing it would one day be needed, never knowing when. She knelt, struck the flint tied around its neck by a cord. The spark flew wildly away. Friya moved forward with cold, controlled fury. She had been in this tunnel many more times than Magan; nothing was new or unusual for her there.

Squinting to see what the younger woman was doing, she steadily drew nearer. Magan struck the flint again. She felt ... what did she feel? Her own passion was gone. It did not beat inside her breast. The desire for vengeance was not there. Nor was the hatred which festered for so long. However, there was a measure of fear, and the high priestess saw it.

Magan struck the flint again, nearer the doll. The grass stuffed inside the dress was dry. This time it caught fire.

"No!"

The cry echoed through the tunnel, lost in the distance. Friya only then realized what was happening. She ran toward Magan, her black hair falling from its binding to flow behind her. Magan placed the smoldering doll on the ground, moved as far as she could to one side. The smoldering herbs filled the tunnel with aromatic smoke, chosen for their magical properties: countering negativity and giving her protection.

Friya stomped on the burning doll. Smoke curled up her gown. Magan moved behind the high priestess who was preoccupied with stamping out the flames. She reached with one arm to encircle the neck of the witch who before seemed invulnerable and tightened her hold. With the other hand, Magan wrenched the witch's medallion free.

Before Magan could pull her hand back, Friya grabbed hold of it, pulling to stretch the arm across her shoulder. She bit the back of Magan's hand and spun around, grabbing at her medallion with her other hand. Magan screamed and used the pain to strengthen her resolve as she jerked the medallion, breaking the chain. She thrust her knee against the back of the witch's knee. Friya's leg gave way and she collapsed. Magan shoved her to the ground. Friya, on all fours, paused to catch her breath. While she regained her balance, Magan ran, putting distance between them. She pressed the stones. Nothing happened. Wrong sequence.

Friya screamed and, steady on her feet now, turned toward her enemy. The turmoil in the witch's mind beat at Magan again, making it impossible to think. Tears flowed down Magan's cheeks, blurring her vision. She tried to focus. Hurry!

Blue, purple, red, green, green, purple. Slip the center stone to the right, press.

Time slowed, and for an instant, it seemed it was the wrong sequence again. She looked into Friya's eyes, near enough to see the fear and hatred shine, then the witch faded from sight.

Magan went to her knees. Sand crunched behind her, a reminder there was a small battle going on and reached to pull the katana from the scabbard. It was a moment before she realized silence filled the air around her. She took two rapid breaths and looked up.

Dzorin stood a few steps away. He smiled wanly, and she relaxed.

"Where in the name of Iah were you? Where is Friya?"

"She's trapped in another plane."

"What?"

"I'll explain later."

"How long will she stay there?"

"I have no idea. Maybe forever."

"Is she alive?"

Magan shook her head. "Yes. I still feel her presence."

If the burdock doll still smoldered, Friya would be severely weakened. Either way, she was trapped. Brynja taught her a woman of such power as the priestess of Mari could not be killed using normal weapons or maneuvers. The best she could do was disable and imprison her until what she was most vulnerable to could be discovered.

Magan and Dzorin stood for the space of several heartbeats, numbed by everything that happened. How long could anyone live in the tunnels? Did they remain young? Would she grow old? She remembered how old the witch had looked the one time she saw her in her true form. Only her magic made her look young and pretty, without parchment skin and hair like straw. One day, Friya would escape. It was inevitable. When she did, she would seek out the one who imprisoned her no matter how old she was.

Magan looked around. Not one sign of fighting, neither warriors nor sound. "How about the others?" she asked.

Dzorin blinked his eyes as if waking. "We were nearly undone when we saw you and Friya disappear. But we managed to hold our ground. I think the loss of the witch startled her mercenaries, too. We beat them back. Two of them are dead, three wounded."

If Friya's disappearance startled her guards, it wasn't because they'd never seen it happen before. They knew how to use the medallions themselves. What surprised them was Magan's using the medallion, probably didn't expect her to have one. Whatever they expected, it most likely wasn't seeing her disappear with Friya following.

"They'll soon be gone," Dzorin stepped around so she could see the post-battle scene. "Lahnlee could not fight at all. His leg is still weak, and he walks with a limp. The survivors will take their dead."

"Did we lose anyone?"

"Leod. Cail is taking it pretty hard. Vanthi was wounded pretty badly. Oh, Lahnlee will take his son's body."

Magan shook her head. "I'm so sorry." Much had happened when she was gone for what seemed to her such a short time.

"Do you think this is the end of it for Lahnlee?" she asked.

Dzorin shrugged. "Who can tell? Maybe, once we get out of here, get back to Sharvik—maybe he won't be able to find us even if he tries."

"I need some water," Magan said. She put her hand on his shoulder and turned toward their camp.

"We have accomplished much, haven't we?" Dzorin said, following.

"I think we have. We've rescued Iah at last. Fought off Friya and Lahnlee."

"But either of them may come back. We will never be completely free of them."

Magan lifted a waterskin, took a deep drink. "I suspect Lahnlee may be satisfied having recovered his son's body," she said, nodding toward the merchant while he wrapped the body in a shroud he brought with him. "As for Friya, she can't get back without this." She held up the medallion. "Perhaps someone will look for her and release her."

"What does it do?"

Magan placed the medallion in his palm. "It was explained to me by Brynja, my teacher, and by Iah in a dream."

They sat on the end of the cart, and she explained the basics of how the medallion worked. She promised to show him one day, after they returned to Sharvik and found peace. He declined to be taught how it worked.

"I've enough of magic for now," he said.

Varas and the others watched five of the witch's guards preparing the wounded and those who survived more or less intact to leave. They gathered up their weapons. One took out a medallion and they disappeared. The bodies of the dead were sent ahead. No one asked where their high priestess was. Nor did they know the combination to find her.

As they rested, and after seeing Friya's guards disappear, Dzorin's curiosity got the better of him and he asked Magan to continue explaining about the alternate planes and how the stones in the medallion could be pressed to move a person from one time or place to another. She stressed how dangerous it could be, how one could get lost and never find the way home and how Brynja showed her the sequence for one plane only and the return. By letting Friya see which one she used, Magan lured the high priestess to follow her into the corridor.

"Once there, I started to burn a small effigy of her. Brynja showed me how to make it using an herb called burdock and a piece of the green cloth you wrapped my hands with. It's old magic, Dzorin. Like knowing someone's name. It's what you used in the dead village when we got out of Mari, wasn't it?"

After escaping from the city, they'd hidden in a village long dead, not knowing ghosts of the long-ago residents were doomed by a curse to roam the place. They could never leave but had the power to avenge themselves on the unwary who wandered into their midst. Those spirits held Dzorin captive until Friya appeared with her guards and they reacted to her and her soldiers as an even bigger threat. He summoned those spirits, and he and Magan escaped while the witch and her guards struggled with the vengeful spirits.

"Yes. A name can give you power over another person. But the doll must give the user a different sort of power."

Magan agreed. "Destroying by fire the one I made to resemble Friya, the smoke protected me and destroyed the negativity she aimed at me. The smoke frightened her so much I was able to take her medallion."

Dzorin shook his head. "There is so much to learn."

She agreed. "Are you sure you won't learn it with me?"

"I don't know, Magan. We'll see. Right now, we help with the wounded and the dead. Then we return to Sharvik as soon as we can."

"Yes, Sharvik. Peace and quiet at last."

When younger, Dzorin trained for the priesthood. He gave it up when he learned of the false magic they used to delude the people. Yet, he had learned real magic, like using someone's real name to manipulate them. She knew the power existed within him, although she'd known him to use it only then. Brynja taught her using the effigy allowed control of a person in very much the same way. But the power of names did not quite work for Magan. Still so much to learn. But would she need to?

They were returning to Sharvik, to the peace and quiet of village life. It was what she wanted most. A chance for the two of them to relax together. *Later,* Magan thought, *we can visit Hattushah.* She'd always wondered what it was like. Maybe they could even go back to Mari someday. Just to see if Friya returned. For now, they would bind their wounds and go home.

CHAPTER 23

"Magan."

The voice coming from outside the door was Julin's. She rushed from the sleep chamber to greet him at the entrance. Maybe he'd come to escort her to Harah's house for the fitting of the marriage dress.

"Garaf wants to see you," he said when she appeared.

"Now?"

Julin nodded. What in the world was this about?

Quickly, she slipped back into the sleep chamber, changed into her best tunic, and rushed with Julin toward the temple. Seven months passed since Iah was returned to the temple. Garaf was now officially high priest, in spite of protests from the people who favored Julin. He was busy these days taking as much power over the people as he could, trying to manipulate the council of elders, most of whom still found it difficult to understand the machinations of power.

It took them over three weeks to make the trek back to Sharvik with Iah in the cart. The wounded warriors moved more slowly and they took their time. The return of the idol to his temple was celebrated for five days with high ceremonies. On the fifth day, Garaf was named high priest, voted into the position by the majority of priests. Garaf was not popular with them or with the people, but he possessed the means to get what he wanted.

The returning warriors were celebrated; Leod was buried with appropriate pomp. His name was listed with those of earlier heroes in the temple. Magan and Dzorin were especially celebrated as the ones who found Iah and made it possible for him to be returned to his home.

In the meantime, Garaf created delay after delay for their wedding. He'd made it clear he didn't approve and would do anything to keep Dzorin from marrying her.

What new excuse had the high priest created against her now? A sudden thought came to her. She stopped and turned to Julin.

"Has something happened to Dzorin?" she asked.

All of the festivities ended days ago. Legitimate reasons came up for postponing the wedding. Finally, the village and the people had settled, the crops were harvested and stored, and tomorrow was her wedding day. Surely nothing would happen to prevent the marriage this close to their moment.

"No."

"What is it then?"

Julin looked angrier than she had ever seen him. She stopped, grabbed the priest's arm, and spun him around to face her.

"Tell me what's going on, Julin."

His eyes held such a look of anguish, it terrified her. After a moment, he looked down. "Garaf does not intend to let you and Dzorin marry."

"Why not?" Her stomach dropped.

Garaf's dislike for her wasn't exactly news, but the two of them worked all these months to overcome every objection and test he threw at them. What else could he do?

"He and some of the other priests have not forgiven you for the night you spent in the temple. You humiliated them by not only surviving but letting everyone in the village know they were not to be feared. Garaf most of all has not forgiven you." He put his hands on her shoulders. "Magan, you've made enemies."

"But after everything we've done."

"He knows you are a woman of power, and a threat to his own; he sees it. You will leave, he hopes."

It was all about her powers and abilities threatening his own.

"Dzorin is with Garaf now," Julin continued. "He's trying to talk Dzorin into abandoning you." He paused again. "Magan, he has been told about the man buried with Iah."

She felt as if someone punched her in the stomach. Who would have told him? Everyone who knew had pledged to never reveal the secret.

"Dzorin will never betray me."

"He loves you. Still, I thought it wise to bring you."

"So, he didn't send for me?"

"No. I . . ."

She turned and ran. They couldn't do this. She'd fought so hard to get Iah back for them. Not for her. For them. *Dzorin, I love you!*

She rushed into the temple and stopped, unsure where to go. Julin came in behind her, grabbed her hand, and led her to the high priest's chamber.

"In there," Julin said at the door.

She threw the door open. Both men looked up.

"Magan!" Dzorin stood and took two steps toward her.

"What are you trying to do, Garaf?" she cried. "We love each other. You can't keep us apart."

"You are an unbeliever," the high priest said. "You committed sacrilege when you buried the soldier with Iah in the sand. Be satisfied we are not banishing you."

So, he did know. Someone told him, in spite of giving his word.

"I can't believe you're doing this," she said. "I did everything possible to get Iah back here, and to get you and everyone else back here. I struggled for more than a year, faced death a number of times. What gives you the right?"

"Iah has denied you permission to marry," Garaf said. "He has not forgiven you."

"That's not true. He doesn't care whether Dzorin and I marry."

"You can't know."

"He told me."

"Liar!" Garaf stood and shook his fist at her. "You blaspheme. Iah would not speak with one such as you. One more word and I *will* banish you." He turned to Dzorin. "Reject her now, Dzorin. Return to the priesthood to expiate the sins you committed with her."

"Dzorin ..." Magan began.

He looked at her, his jaw muscles taut, his hands tightened into fists. Clearly, he was angry but at whom? She forgot to breathe, fear caught in her throat.

Magan stepped around him to grab the high priest by the collar of his robe.

"I am not answerable to you," she said with her nose inches away from his. "One more word and I will see to it Sharvik needs another high priest."

She pushed Garaf into his chair. He cowered there, speechless for several heartbeats.

"Dzorin, you were a priest once," Garaf screamed. "Defend your god and your high priest. Kill her."

"You ungrateful little man," Dzorin said. "You may be high priest, but it was not at my urging." He took Magan's hand and started toward the door. "We will decide whether or not we live here in Sharvik. Married or unmarried."

He pulled her out of the room, stopping short when he spied Julin lurking in the shadows.

"Will you truly leave Sharvik?" the priest asked.

"Maybe," Magan said. Dzorin nodded. "If we do, would you like to come with us? We'll have high adventures."

"Ah, no. Too old am I for adventuring. Besides," he continued, "someone will have to stay behind and try to soften the blow of Garaf's influence over our people." He clapped Dzorin on the shoulder and smiled at Magan. "I will come see you tonight."

"Thank you, Julin," Magan said. She kissed him on the cheek, then she and Dzorin rushed out into the sunlight. They stood on the temple steps outside the door, holding tightly to each other's hand. Dzorin quivered with anger. His grip was so tight the bones in her own scraped together, the pain steadying her. Tears of frustration stung her eyes. She had never believed the priests would go so far.

So much had happened in this courtyard. The battle with the raiders when they made off with the idol. Training with Brynja. Loving with Dzorin. This was their home. They fought for the people, fought to bring Iah home. Garaf was an ungrateful wretch, terrified her presence would undermine his authority.

But what could they do? Garaf was high priest and ever since the sojourn in Hattushah, he gathered more and more authority into his hands. With the support of the priests and the weakness of the elders, his was the final word.

They walked and she concentrated on the physical pain rather than the pain in her soul. With her vision blurred with tears, she let herself be led, not caring where, as long as it was Dzorin who led the way.

Back at her house, she paced while he sat brooding over the morning's events. He sat silent and still, his anger palpable in the small space.

"Damn him!" she shouted. "Damn him." She strode the length of the room twice more.

"What must I do to make these people accept me?" she said. "How can we stay here, Dzorin? If we do—and I have no intention of not living together—you will be ostracized along with me." She knelt in front of him.

"Can you live with the fact we could never return? It's the way it would be if we leave now. You know it's true. Sharvik is more home to you than it has ever been to me. But as long as Garaf lives, we cannot return."

Tears ran down his cheeks and he swallowed, his Adam's apple bobbing.

"How much more can we endure?" she said. "I will go without you if you choose to stay, but I will not live in Sharvik any longer. I cannot."

"I can't live without you," he said. "If you leave ... oh, god, why must we make this decision? Maybe the people ..."

"They won't go against the high priest, especially not one chosen by Amleth as his successor. Even if *some* of them would be willing to fight him on our behalf, I could not allow it. The people have suffered so much. Internal strife could tear Sharvik apart." Garaf had produced what was supposed to be Amleth's wishes on the matter, written on a clay tablet. She didn't believe it was real, but others could not, or would not, challenge it.

"It truly matters to you what happens to ..." he began.

"... my people," she finished. "Yes, it matters. Even though they rejected me in the past because I'm different. Even though I will never see them again, it matters. We are of the same blood."

"Theirs is thinner than yours, Magan. Ah, the adventures we will have."

He stood and took both her hands in his, pulling her to her

feet, held her gaze with his. Her love for him burned in her belly and her breast. It took her breath away. The sound of his voice could make her forget where she was and what she was doing. Such love was an adventure in itself.

For two days, they talked about where they could go and what they wanted to see of the known world. They both wanted to see the sea, he for the second time. They spoke to the few in the village who journeyed so far—and it was far, they were told. It was many days away, but there were villages to visit between Sharvik and there. Wonderful cities stood on the edge of the world from which many of the goods they needed and used came in wooden ships with sails.

Winter was a difficult time with wind and storms, but spring would soon arrive. With so many villages along the way, finding shelter would not be a problem. Julin especially emphasized this. He spent many hours with them, helping them plan and prepare.

They packed as much as they could carry: water, food and a few clothes. The weapons they would need. She chose the katana and her bronze sword. He, his bronze sword and the wonderful knife Lahnlee gave him. He thought about leaving it behind, but it had become such a part of him and couldn't bring himself to give it up.

On one of his many visits, Julin told them Garaf ordered Varas to run them out of Sharvik, which the captain refused to do. It was as far as the old warrior would go, though. Julin had hoped he might insist on the two warriors being given the honors due them, but his nature was always to obey not to rebel. The spurt of command, other than militarily, in organizing the villagers' return seemed to be the one and only.

Many villagers gladly gave them whatever supplies they needed for the journey, some even saying how sorry they were to see them leave. Not one voiced the same objections to the high priest.

Their last night, Julin came to their quarters. With Sher and Cain as witnesses, the priest said the words binding the lovers together. The unofficial ceremony didn't have the same authority as it would if the high priest said the words and anointed them with oil in front of the golden Iah. On the other hand, it meant more than anything Garaf could have said or done.

The priest was the only one who walked them to the gates five days after Garaf made his pronouncement. The two of them stood with Julin outside of the gates, staring beyond the Diyala, into the desert. They'd stood there several times before, looking forward, on their way in service to their people. The world awaited, both inviting and frightening. Would this time be better? The first time they were chasing something. This time—well, they were either running from something or toward something. Maybe the lack of a defined goal wasn't a good omen, but it was all they had.

"May Iah smile upon you," Julin said. It was the usual blessing from the priests.

Magan looked at him, surprised to see tears in his eyes. "I thought everything was going to be good once we returned from Hattushah," she said. He shook his head.

"Thank you for everything," Dzorin said. The two men embraced.

"Things will be a little dull around here," the priest said as he embraced Magan. "Love one another."

He turned and walked back into the village with bowed head. Watching him, Magan realized someone stood in the shadows of the wall.

"It's Sher," she said, waving. The warrior waved back, then he, too, turned and walked away.

She adjusted her pack and turned to face the desert. It was difficult to shake the feeling this was all her fault. Someday, Dzorin might hate her for making him leave his home.

"Are you certain?" she said.

"Let's go," he said. "Adventure awaits."

"Dzorin, are you sure?" she repeated.

"My life is with you," he said. "And out there."

It was time to go. Don't look back. Only forward. Just the two of them.

ABOUT THE AUTHOR

Cary Osborne's tastes have always been eclectic, due to her varied background. Because of that, she has written in several genres, including science fiction, fantasy, and horror. Recently, she delved into the fictional world of mysteries. She won an honorable mention and was a finalist in the Writers of the Future Contest for short stories. After living all over the country, she recently moved from New Mexico to settle in Oklahoma.

Book List:

The Iroshi Trilogy
Iroshi
The Glaive
Persea

The Deathweave Series
Deathweave
Darkloom

The Sydney St. John Mysteries
Oklahoma Winds
Black Ice
Saving Souls

Fantasy Works
Winter Queen
When God Was Stolen Book 1

Curious about other Crossroad Press books?
Stop by our site:
http://www.crossroadpress.com
We offer quality writing
in digital, audio, and print formats.